# He held cynical glitter in his eye.

'You need to grow up, Kitty,' he said. 'You're a young, fanciful girl in a woman's body. Life isn't a fairytale. There are no handsome princes out there who'll declare undying love for you and carry you off into the sunset. There are no fairy godmothers to make everything turn out right in the end. There are no genies in bottles, no magic spells, and sure as hell there are precious few happy-ever-afters.'

Kitty folded her arms imperiously. 'Are you done?'

The air crackled with electric tension as dark blue eyes warred with grey.

'No,' he said, his eyes glittering as he closed the distance between them in one stride. 'Not quite.'

She gave a little startled gasp as his strong hands gripped her by the upper arms, pulling her to him. Her body jolted with sensual energy when it came into contact with his. It was like a dead battery being plugged into a power source. Currents of energy flowed through her, kick-starting her senses into throbbing, pulsing life. His mouth came down and blazed with furnace-hot heat against hers. As the kiss progressed in intensity raw need licked along her flesh like trails of runaway fire. Desire pooled in her belly, hot and liquid, melting her to the backbone. His tongue thrust boldly into her mouth, commanding and conquering, demanding and deliciously, dangerously male.

## Dear Reader

While I was writing my last Medical Romance™, THE SURGEON SHE NEVER FORGOT, I had a scene where an Accident and Emergency doctor came in to talk to my hero Lewis Beck about his ill father. I found my next medical hero Jake Chandler right then and there. I just love it when characters come to me and beg me to write their story!

Jake was tall and incredibly good-looking, with dark blue eyes. I knew immediately that he was a bit of a playboy. I even knew *why* he was so against settling down. His backstory was like a download in my head.

All I needed now was a suitable heroine to rock Jake's world. And in no time at all newly qualified A&E doctor Kitty Cargill came along. Again it was like a download. I knew immediately that Kitty would be a classic fish out of water. I also knew she would be an old-fashioned English girl from an unconventional background.

A sweetheart, a home girl with a broken heart, meets a commitment-phobe, notoriously sexy playboy. What a perfect mix for a pulse-racing romance!

I love writing the scene where my characters meet for the first time. I have so much fun thinking of ways they can take an instant dislike to each other, or get the wrong impression, or strike passionate sparks from the first moment their eyes meet. Jake and Kitty certainly didn't let me down. Kitty makes a first impression on Jake that is nothing like the impression she hoped to make on her devilishly handsome boss!

I hope you enjoy reading about how Jake and Kitty met and fell in love, and that you laugh and cry with them along the way. I certainly did!

Warmest wishes

*Melanie Milburne*

# DR CHANDLER'S SLEEPING BEAUTY

BY
MELANIE MILBURNE

*To Andrea Debomford, who gave me the inspiration*
*for the way Jake and Kitty first meet.*
*Thanks for your friendship. Love you. xxx*

First published in Great Britain 2012
by Mills & Boon, an imprint of Harlequin (UK) Limited.
Large Print edition 2013
Harlequin (UK) Limited, Eton House,
18-24 Paradise Road, Richmond, Surrey TW9 1SR

© Melanie Milburne 2012

ISBN: 978 0 263 23105 2

Harlequin (UK) policy is to use papers that are
natural, renewable and recyclable products and made
from wood grown in sustainable forests. The logging
and manufacturing process conform to the legal
environmental regulations of the country of origin.

Printed and bound in Great Britain
by CPI Antony Rowe, Chippenham, Wiltshire

From as soon as **Melanie Milburne** could pick up a pen she knew she wanted to write. It was when she picked up her first Mills and Boon® at seventeen that she realised she wanted to write romance. After being distracted for a few years by meeting and marrying her own handsome hero, surgeon husband Steve, and having two boys, plus completing a Masters of Education and becoming a nationally ranked athlete (masters swimming), she decided to write. Five submissions later she sold her first book, and is now a multi-published, award-winning, *USA TODAY* bestselling author. In 2008 she won the Australian Readers Association most popular category/series romance, and in 2011 she won the prestigious Romance Writers of Australia R*BY award.

Melanie loves to hear from her readers via her website www.melaniemilburne.com.au, or on Facebook http://www.facebook.com/pages/ Melanie-Milburne/351594482609

**Recent titles by the same author:**

SYDNEY HARBOUR HOSPITAL:
  LEXI'S SECRET*
THE SURGEON SHE NEVER FORGOT
THE MAN WITH THE LOCKED AWAY HEART

**Sydney Harbour Hospital*

**These books are also available in eBook format from www.millsandboon.co.uk**

Praise for Melanie Milburne,
who also writes for
Mills & Boon® Modern™ Romance:

'A classic romance with great characters
and sensual dialogue that will raise your
temperature as the love story
makes you laugh and cry.'
—*RT Book Reviews* on
HIS POOR LITTLE RICH GIRL

Melanie Milburne's
*Surrendering All But Her Heart*
is also out this month
in Mills & Boon Modern™ Romance!

# CHAPTER ONE

'I CAN'T believe you talked me into wearing this,' Kitty Cargill said to her cousin as they entered the city hotel where Julie's 'Pimps and Prostitutes' fancy dress thirtieth birthday party was being held. 'I'm sure it's because I'm still suffering from jet lag and I'm not in my right mind.'

'You look awesome,' Julie said. 'I never knew you had such great legs. That PVC skirt really shows some serious thigh.'

Kitty pulled the skirt—which in her opinion was too skimpy even to qualify for the term—down over the ladder in the black fishnet tights that her cousin had insisted was an essential part of the get-up. 'Now I can see where my mother got her wacky out-there genes,' she said, cringing in embarrassment at some of the looks she was attracting as they made their way to the function room.

'Lighten up, hon,' Julie said. 'You're not going to last long in Aussieland unless you strap on a sense of humour. You're way too conservative. You Brits all act like you've been potty-trained at gunpoint.'

'Ha, ha, ha,' Kitty said. 'I'll have you know I wasn't potty-trained at all. My parents thought it was far more progressive and fundamental to my development that I sorted it all out for myself when I was good and ready.'

Julie grinned at her. 'So should I be worried about you going where you shouldn't while you're bunking down with me?'

Kitty gave her a look. 'Don't worry,' she said. 'I won't be with you much longer. I've already found a town house to rent online. The real estate agent confirmed it this afternoon. It's not far from the hospital and even closer to the beach at Bondi.'

'It sounds perfect,' Julie said. 'Have you met anyone from St Benedict's yet? Your boss in A&E or the CEO?'

'Not yet,' Kitty said. 'I'm going to introduce myself in the next day or so. I'm not due to start until next week, but I thought it'd be polite to put in an appearance—given I didn't go through the normal face-to-face interview process.'

'I still can't quite get my head around you being a fully-fledged doctor,' Julie said, giving her a playful shoulder-bump. 'Last time I saw you, when Mum and I came to London for Christmas, you were playing with dolls.'

*Life was certainly a whole lot simpler then*, Kitty thought wistfully as she followed her cousin into the party room, which was thumping with deafening music.

Jake Chandler was on night shift for the fourth night in a row and feeling it. Friday and Saturday nights were not his favourite times to be on duty. Far too many partygoers with too much alcohol on board and too little common sense clogged public A&E departments like his all over the country. In their noisy midst were the seriously sick and injured.

So far tonight he'd had to deal with the death of a sixteen-year-old girl in a motorcycle accident and a serious stabbing. The girl had been riding pillion on the back of her boyfriend's bike. It had been her first time on a motorbike and her second date with the boyfriend. She had been the only child of a single mother. Jake could still see the collapse of the girl's mother's face when he had told her.

The stabbing had been a drug deal turned sour. The guy had almost bled out before Jake could stem the bleeding. The guy was twenty-four years old—the same age as Jake's younger brother, Robbie. Would this be how *his* kid brother ended up? Found in some sleazy back alley, mortally wounded, stoned and senseless? How could he stop it? What more could he do? Robbie's refusal to grow up and take responsibility for himself made Jake feel he had failed.

He had let his family down.

*He had let his mother down.*

Jake glanced at the clock on the wall on his way back from escorting the stabbing victim to Theatre.

Five minutes to midnight.

It was about time for the drunk and disorderly

to come spilling in. He just hoped Robbie wasn't one of them.

'Dr Chandler?' Jake's registrar Lei Chung approached him while he was washing his hands at one of the sterilising basins. 'I have a couple of tipsy call girls in Bay Five. One of them has a suspected broken ankle.'

Jake mentally rolled his eyes as he tugged some paper towels out to dry his hands. 'They *told* you they were call girls?' he asked.

'They didn't have to,' Lei said, rolling his eyes. 'Just wait until you see them.'

'They're entitled to the same level of care as anyone else,' Jake said, tossing the screwed-up paper in the bin before reaching for a new pair of gloves. 'Have you ordered an X-ray?'

'The radiographer will be down in ten minutes,' Lei said. 'He's seeing a patient on the orthopaedic ward. One of his hip patients had a fall.'

Jake twitched the curtain aside of Bay Five. 'Hello,' he said. 'I'm Dr Chandler.'

The girl sitting beside the one lying on the trolley shot to her feet. 'I'm so terribly sorry about this,' she said, speaking in a cut-glass London accent that didn't fool Jake for a moment. 'I don't think it's broken. I'm sure it's just a sprain. But my cousin is in so much pain I thought we should have it X-rayed. I thought it best if—'

Jake quirked one brow upwards. 'Your... cousin?'

'Her name is Julie Banning, and I'm—'

'Hello, Julie,' Jake said, turning to the girl on the trolley. 'Can you tell me what happened?'

'I was dancing with this guy and his legs got twisted with mine,' Julie said, with an Australian accent even broader than his. 'I hit the floor and twisted my ankle. I heard something snap— I swear to God I did. It hurts like freaking hell.'

'Let's have a look, shall we?' Jake said.

He examined the ankle, but found only swelling and tenderness over the lateral ligaments and no obvious fracture. He checked the patient for any other injuries, but apart from a bruise on her elbow she was all clear—which was lucky considering how much alcohol he could smell on her and her posh-sounding little sidekick.

'I'll order an X-ray just to be on the safe side,'

he said. 'An orderly will be with you shortly. And go easy on the partying, OK? You could've really done some serious damage. You might not be so lucky next time.' He gave the other young woman a cursory nod and left the cubicle.

'Dr Chandler?' The young woman spoke from behind him just as he got to his office.

Jake turned to look at her. 'Yes?'

She shifted her weight from foot to foot, looking distinctly uncomfortable. He didn't know working girls *could* blush. Maybe she was new to the game. She didn't look very old. Her skin was porcelain-smooth and her eyes—in spite of the heavy eyeshadow—were clear and bright and a rather stunning shade of grey. Perhaps she was worried he was going to ask for a drug screen on her 'cousin', or a blood alcohol level.

'I wanted to say thank you for seeing my cousin so promptly,' she said. 'I was worried it might take hours and hours. She seemed in a lot of pain and I—'

'Do you realise the dangers of binge drinking?' Jake asked, frowning at her reproachfully.

Her eyes flickered. 'Pardon?'

He stripped her with his gaze. 'You smell like a brewery, the both of you.'

Her cheeks flushed bright red. 'I'm not drunk!'

He rolled his eyes in disdain. 'Yeah, that's what they all say.'

'But I'm not!' she said. 'Julie spilt her drink on the floor when she fell. I knelt down to help her and got soaked in it. I've only had half a glass of champagne the whole night.'

'How much has your cousin had to drink?' he asked.

'A bit…' She bit her bottom lip. 'A lot…quite a lot…loads, actually. It's her thirtieth birthday. I told her to slow down but she wouldn't listen.' She made a self-deprecating movement of her mouth. 'She thinks I'm too conservative.'

Jake flicked his gaze over her sinfully short PVC skirt and the black bustier top that show-cased a rack that was small but no less impressive. 'I can see what she means,' he said dryly.

Her big grey eyes with their raccoon-like eye-shadow widened in affront and her small neat chin came up. 'Dr Chandler, perhaps I should take this opportunity to properly introduce myself,' she said. 'My name is Kitty Car—'

'Kitty as in Kitty Litter?' Jake put in, without holding back on his mocking smile.

Her generously plumped mouth flattened. 'No,' she said, those storm cloud eyes flashing at him resentfully. 'Kitty as in Katherine. Katherine Cargill. *Dr* Katherine Cargill, to be precise.'

Jake rocked back on his heels. So *this* was the new three-month appointment who had been recruited while he'd been away on leave. He'd been wrong about the accent. Funny, but he'd thought it way too posh to be for real. Maybe it was time to have a little fun. Let her get to know the colonial natives, so to speak. God knew he could do with a bit of a laugh after the night he'd had.

'Have things got so bad in the public health system that junior doctors have to moonlight in other less salubrious professions?' he asked.

She glared at him. 'This is not what it looks like,' she said, waving a stiff hand to encompass her attire. 'It's a *costume*.'

Jake leisurely ran his gaze over every inch of her outfit, right down her long shapely legs encased in sexy fishnets to the scarily high heels on her dainty feet. 'It's very convincing,' he said.

She frowned at him. 'Haven't you been to a fancy dress party before?'

'Yeah,' he drawled. 'I went as the Big Bad Wolf. I huffed and I puffed and brought the whole house down.'

She gave him a haughty look down the length of her nose that was right out the pages of a Jane Austen novel. 'At least you wouldn't have had to go to the trouble and expense of hiring a costume,' she said. 'You would have gone just as you are.'

Jake held her feisty little eye-lock. He felt a stirring in his groin that had nothing to do with her skimpy outfit. There was something about her imperious air and her toffee-nosed accent that made his flesh tingle from head to foot.

Was it his self-imposed dating drought that had stirred his senses so intensely? He'd made a bet with his sister at Christmas that he could give up sex for the rest of the summer. Rosie had criticised his playboy lifestyle, even going as far as saying it was setting a bad example for her young son, Nathan. If he lost the bet he would have to pay Rosie a thousand dollars towards Nathan's education fund. He had no problem with donating the money for Nathan. He would give that and more, bet or no bet. But he *did* have a problem with his kid sister thinking he had no self-control and discipline. So he'd set a new record for himself—a new personal best. He didn't like admitting it, but abstinence had been good for him. His sex life *had* become a bit boring and predictable over the last year. But he didn't want anything long-term. He was happy with his fancy-free approach to relationships. It had just been a bad year, that was all.

Besides, he *liked* his flings short and uncomplicated.

No strings.

No rings.

No promises.

Once his period of celibacy was up, Kitty Cargill, with her I'm-just-pretending-to-be-a-wild-child routine, could be just the one to kick things off for the rest of this year.

'You can take your cousin home as soon as

she's had her X-ray,' Jake said. 'And I hope when I next see you in this unit you're wearing something a little more appropriate. We're supposed to be saving patients' lives here, not giving them myocardial infarcts. Understood?'

She gave him a glittering glare. 'Perfectly, Dr Chandler.'

*'Grrrgghhh!'* Kitty was still fuming as she unpacked her things at her new town house three days later. She cringed in embarrassment when she thought of turning up for work the following Monday. How on earth was she going to face him?

Julie, damn her, was *still* laughing about it, in spite of hobbling about on crutches and having to take time off from her job as a beautician. Her cousin thought the sprained ankle was worth it to have seen someone as prim and proper as Kitty floundering so far out of her depth.

'God, he was *so* gorgeous,' Julie had said only that morning when Kitty had rung to check on her. 'Did you see how dark his blue eyes were?

And so tall! He must have been six foot three or four, don't you think?'

'I'm trying *not* to think about him,' Kitty said. 'That was singularly the most excruciatingly embarrassing evening of my entire life.' *Well, apart from finding my best friend, Sophie, in bed with my long-term boyfriend the very weekend I thought he was going to propose to me.* 'I wonder if it's too late to ask for a transfer to another hospital…' She bit down on her lip, daunted at the thought of finding a new placement at such short notice.

'He had great hands,' Julie rabbited on. 'So strong and capable and masculine. I wonder if he's married. I don't think he was wearing a ring. But he was wearing gloves, so who knows? Maybe a little fling with your new boss will be just the trick to get that two-timing jerk Charles Wetherby out of your system once and for all.'

'Will you stop it, for pity's sake?' Kitty said. 'I don't want to talk about Dr Chandler.' *Or Charles*, she added silently, with a tight cramping pain over her heart.

But even so her mind kept rerunning the

whole debacle like a DVD-player jammed on replay. Jake Chandler had accused her of being drunk and yet she was more or less a teetotaller. He'd thought she was a prostitute, and yet she was twenty-six years old and had only had one lover—her childhood sweetheart, who had turned out not to be such a sweetheart after all.

This three-month trip Down Under was part of her coping strategy.

Kitty had always considered herself a gracious and forgiving type, but staying in London while Charles got married to Sophie Hamilton was stretching the bounds of her grace and forgiveness a little too far.

Kitty had grown up with Charles. He had lived in the same village, on the same street, in a house only four doors down from hers. She had gone through infants, primary school, high school and medical school with him. They had done their residency and internship at the same hospitals. They had practically been joined at the hip. Everyone had described them as the perfect couple. They'd never argued. They'd been best friends. They'd enjoyed the same things. They'd had the same friends. They had wanted the same things—or so Kitty had thought.

For months she had been expecting a romantic proposal. She had even secretly chosen a ring to match the promise ring Charles had given her on her sixteenth birthday. She had walked into bridal shops and dreamily tried on gorgeous gowns and voluminous veils. She had bought dozens of bridal magazines, making copious notes as she flicked through them. She had even—she cringed in embarrassment even now—gone to several wedding venues to check on prices and availability.

Now Charles was gone and she was on her own.

No perfect white wedding.

No honeymoon in a luxurious and exotic location.

*No happy ever after.*

Kitty worked on flattening cardboard boxes for the recycling bin in the town house complex car park. She was hot and sweaty. She wondered if she would ever get used to this oppressively humid heat. Just as well she was only staying twelve weeks. London could get hot in summer, but Sydney in early February was like living in a pizza oven. She had been to the beach, but the sun—in spite of layers of sunscreen—had scorched her pale skin and given her even more freckles on her nose. Tendrils of her thick chestnut hair were sticking to her neck, even though she had piled it as high as she could in a ponytail-cum-knot on the top of her head.

She brushed her forearm across her perspiring brow and reached for the last box. The last box, however, was reluctant to be reduced to a flat layer. She stomped on it, but it flapped back up to snap at her ankles. 'Down, down, *down*, damn you to sodding hell and back,' she cursed, and she gave it one last almighty stomp by jumping on it with both feet.

'Need some help?' A deep male voice drawled from behind her.

Kitty swung around so fast she almost lost her footing. Her eyes went wide and her heart gave a flap like a sail in a fifty-knot wind. *'You!'* she gasped.

He gave a sweeping obsequious bow. 'At your service, ma'am.'

Kitty felt her skin pebble all over with irritation and embarrassment. 'I was just—' She waved her hand at the recycling bin. 'Um…recycling…'

His eyes were smiling, no—*laughing* at her. 'Looks like you need a man to do that for you,' he said.

'I do *not* need a man.' She felt the slow burn of Jake Chandler's gaze as it took in her baggy track pants and tank top, pausing for a heart-stopping moment on her breasts. Her stomach felt as if it was being stirred by a long-handled spoon and her heart kept leaping and jumping as if it was being prodded by the wire of a high-voltage electric current.

She couldn't remember Charles ever looking at her like that—as if he could see right through her clothes to the flesh beneath. She couldn't remember feeling so taken aback by a man's looks before, either. She had to admit Jake Chandler had looked pretty hot in theatre scrubs on Saturday night, but dressed in dark blue jeans and a white T-shirt he looked staggeringly gorgeous. The white of the T-shirt highlighted his naturally olive-toned skin, and his perfectly formed pectoral muscles and flat, toned stomach indicated he was a man who worked hard and played harder. He was certainly every bit as tall as Julie had suggested, and because Kitty wasn't wearing four-inch heels she had to crane her neck to meet his dark sapphire-blue eyes.

'Are you the new tenant?' he asked.

'Yes, I'm renting number three,' she said, with the sort of cool composure that would have earned her an Oscar if she were an actor. But she certainly didn't feel cool around Jake Chandler. She felt blisteringly hot, and it didn't have a thing to do with the searing temperature of the summer day. There was something about his dark blue gaze that made her feel as if each time he looked at her he wasn't seeing her as she was dressed now but as she had been dressed the other night. 'Don't let me keep you,' she said, bending down to scoop up the recalcitrant cardboard.

'Here,' he said, reaching for the bundle that was almost as tall as her. 'Let me help you with that.'

Kitty felt one of his hands brush against her right breast in the exchange. It was like a strike of lightning against her flesh. It zapped right through her body, sizzling it with erotic heat and making every hair on her head rise up from her scalp. She stepped back as if she had been burnt, her face flaming, her heart going at a pace that would have made any decent cardiologist call for an immediate ECG.

But Jake Chandler seemed totally unaffected. He stuffed the cardboard into the bin and shoved it down as if it were a marshmallow with a powerful press of his muscled and deeply tanned arm. 'Do you need anything else done?' he asked. 'Furniture shifted? Boxes carried up the stairs?' His dark blue eyes glinted again. 'Costumes unpacked—that sort of thing?'

'I'm fine… Thank you,' she said, wishing she could stop blushing like a silly little schoolgirl. What was it about this man that made her feel so gauche? Was it his laughing blue eyes or his in-your-face masculinity or both? 'You've done quite enough.'

A tiny silence crept past as he continued to hold her flustered gaze with his unwavering one.

'I'm having a few people over for a barbecue this evening,' he said. 'Nothing fancy. No cucumber sandwiches or anything. Just a few steaks and snags slapped on the grill and some beers. Feel free to pop over and join us.'

Kitty thought of the frozen, calorie-controlled, most probably hideously tasteless dinner she had bought. She thought of eating it alone, just like all the other frozen meals she had mechanically consumed with tears on the side since the breakup. She hadn't seen the point in cooking for one person so she had stopped.

But then she thought of spending the evening with Jake Chandler and his coterie of likeminded beer-swilling friends. What if some of them were other staff members from St Benedict's? He was probably only inviting her so he could make fun of her in front of them. She had met his type before: the confident, smoothtalking charmer who was the life of every party.

*She would be roasted alive.*

'Thank you for the invitation, but I think I'll pass,' she said.

'I hope we don't keep you awake,' he said. 'I wasn't expecting anyone to move in for another week or two. The people between your house and mine are overseas. Feel free to pop over if you change your mind or find yourself at a loose end.'

'Thank you, but no,' she said, even more crisply this time.

His dark eyes twinkled again. 'Social diary that full already, is it?' he asked.

She sent him a flinty look. 'Packed,' she said, and turned and left.

At just before midnight Kitty stuck her head under the pillow for the tenth time but it didn't make a single bit of difference. The *doof-doof* of Jake Chandler's sound system reverberated through her building. He was on the opposite side of the complex but it felt as if he was in the next room. She was surprised no one else had complained, but then she remembered the other occupants were away on a trip overseas.

She threw the pillow aside and stomped over to the window overlooking the small courtyard that separated their town houses. She could see people drinking and dancing in Jake's living room. All the lights were blaring and the appetising smell of steak and sausages and onions was still lingering in the air. The sight of all that fun going on was a cruel reminder of her aching loneliness. She hated feeling so bitter, but how could she help it? Everywhere she looked people were acting as if they had not a care in the world.

Didn't Jake Chandler have to show up for work in the morning? What was he thinking, partying on as if there was no tomorrow? So much for his sanctimonious lecture on binge drinking. What a hypocrite!

Kitty decided there was only one way to attack and that was on the front line. She ditched her nightwear and dressed in her track pants and a shapeless cotton shirt and slipped her feet into a pair of flip-flops. It wasn't sophisticated or glamorous, but at this ungodly hour she didn't give a damn.

\* \* \*

'Wasn't that the doorbell?' asked Rosie, Jake's younger sister, her eyes brightening with hope. 'Maybe Robbie decided to come after all.'

Jake gave her shoulder a gentle squeeze. 'Don't get your hopes up, kiddo,' he said. 'You know what he's like. He probably won't even remember it's your birthday.'

'Yeah, what was I thinking?' Rosie's shoulders dropped resignedly and she made her way back to her friends.

Jake let out a quick sigh before he turned to open the door to find his cute posh little neighbour standing there. 'Hey,' he said flashing her a smile. 'You changed your mind. Do you want a beer?'

'Your music is keeping me awake,' she said, sending him an arctic look. 'I would very much appreciate it if you would turn it down.'

Jake ran his gaze over her pretty girl-next-door face with its cloud of chestnut hair that was currently looking more bird's nest than brushed. Her cheeks had two spots of bright red on them and her plump pink mouth was pushed forward in a pout. 'My kind of music not your thing, huh?' he said. He leant indolently against the doorjamb, one ankle crossed over the other, as he rubbed at the regrowth on his jaw. 'Let me guess… Classical, right?'

Her gunmetal-grey eyes flashed at him. 'I hardly see how my taste in music has anything to do with you,' she said.

'It will if you play the violin at all hours of the day and night.' He narrowed his eyes at her enquiringly. 'You don't, do you? Play the violin, I mean.'

She gave a little shuffle from foot to foot, as if the ground beneath her feet had suddenly become too hot to stand on. 'What do you have against the violin?' she asked, looking at him with an equally narrow-eyed look.

'I knew it!' he said, thumping the doorjamb with the flat of his palm in victory. 'It was either that or the viola or the cello. You don't strike me as a woodwind or brass girl. Strings are your thing.'

'And I suppose no strings is yours?' she returned, with an arch of one of her brows.

'How'd you guess?' Jake said, grinning.

Her eyes gave a disparaging little roll. 'I can recognise a player at three paces,' she said.

'We're not talking about musical instruments, are we?' he asked.

Her mouth tightened primly, reminding him of his kindergarten teacher when he'd brought a dead mouse in for Show and Tell.

'I'm not interested in what you do in your private life,' she said. 'You can play as hard and as often as you like.'

'Oh, I always play hard and often,' Jake drawled, watching in amusement as her face deepened even more in a blush as she realised her unintentional *double entendre*.

'I can see there is no point in continuing this discussion,' she said in a starchy tone. 'But let me tell you: your puerile sense of humour is not what I was expecting in an A&E director.'

Jake looked down at her uptilted heart-shaped face with its glorious crown of tousled hair. He could smell the sweet, old-fashioned but delightful white lilac scent of her shampoo. It danced around his nostrils, teasing them into an involuntary flare. He could see the tiny dusting of freckles on the aristocratic slope of her nose. He could see her currently pursed but tempting full-lipped mouth.

He felt lust hit him in his gut like a closed-fist punch coming out of nowhere.

He wanted to bend down and cover those lips and feel them soften and swell beneath his. He wanted to taste the silk of her skin, to run his hands over the gentle slope of her breasts to see if they felt as soft and gorgeous as they looked. He wanted to feel her hands on him, their softness exploring his hardness. He wanted her to come down off that high horse of hers and ride him instead.

*Whoa, there*. He slammed the brakes on his thoughts. He had a whole month to go before he cashed in on the bet with his sister. The shortest month, admittedly, but it could prove to be the longest—especially if Kitty Cargill kept turning up in front of him looking so hot and sexy and combative.

'I can't say you're quite what I was expecting, either,' he said.

Her brows knitted together over her eyes. 'What do you mean by that?'

Jake allowed himself a quick study of her mouth before he met her gaze. 'I had a read-through of your application,' he said. 'I was away when the acting director approved your appointment.'

Her slim throat rose and fell, the action like a small creature wriggling under a carpet. 'And?' she said.

'I noted that you'd failed the practical on your ATLs,' he said.

Her small white teeth nibbled at her bottom lip. 'Yes... I'm thinking about doing the Australian equivalent while I'm here,' she said.

'I expect every member of my team to be on top of their game,' Jake said. 'There's an EMST course I'm directing in a month's time. There might be a space left if you contact the course co-ordinator, otherwise book in to do the next available one.'

'I'll look into it,' she said.

'What made you come all the way out to Australia for three months?' he asked.

Her eyes moved slightly to the left of his. 'It seemed like a good opportunity to get to know my aunt and uncle and three cousins who live here,' she said. 'I hadn't seen them in a while. Years, actually.'

Jake nodded towards her town house. 'You bring anyone with you?' he asked. 'Boyfriend? Partner?'

A flush came over her cheeks and her eyes moved away from his. 'No.'

His eyes went to her left hand, where a pretty little ring rested. 'Is that just for show or is there a fiancé waiting for you back in England?'

She twirled the ring on her finger with her thumb. 'I'm not engaged,' she said. 'This is a—'

'Let me guess,' Jake said, flashing her another quick grin. 'A costume?'

She gave him a gimlet glare. 'It's a promise ring,' she said. 'I got it when I was sixteen. I can't get it off.'

'You could have it cut off,' Jake said. 'Or would that be breaking the promise?'

She frowned at him. 'Is this inquisition really necessary?'

He gave a negligent shrug. 'Just making con-versation,' he said. 'You sure you wouldn't like a drink? I'll get the gang to turn the music down. I might even be able to find some Vivaldi or something on the playlist on my iPod.'

'Please don't put yourself out on my behalf,' she said, sending him another one of her icy looks. 'Goodnight, Dr Chandler.'

'Goodnight, Dr Cargill,' Jake said, but she had already stalked back across the courtyard.

# CHAPTER TWO

'AND this is the staff tea room,' Gwen Harold, the unit's ward clerk, informed Kitty on Monday morning. 'There's a larger doctors' room upstairs, but the lifts are so busy that by the time you get there it's almost time to get back. Dr Chandler organised this little room for us instead. Have you met him yet?'

'Um…yes,' Kitty said, trying not to blush. 'A couple of times now.'

Gwen smiled. 'He's a fabulous director,' she said. 'He's tough, but fair. And he's got a great sense of humour. I've worked with a lot of A&E directors in my time but Jake's the best by a long shot. The way I see it, we have enough drama coming through the doors without adding to it with rants and raves from the top. Jake's always cool in a crisis. Never seen him lose his temper—not even with the junior staff.'

'He sounds like the perfect boss,' Kitty said with a forced smile.

'Oh, he's got his faults,' Gwen said. 'He's quite the playboy. I don't think he's ever had a relationship last longer than a couple of months. A heartbreaker, that's what he is.' She gave Kitty a little wink. 'Don't say I didn't warn you.'

'Thanks for the warning, but my heart is quite safe,' Kitty said in a self-assured tone.

'Got someone back in England?' Gwen asked.

'No,' Kitty said. 'Not any more.'

'Never mind, dear,' Gwen said, patting Kitty on the arm. 'Plenty more fish in the sea, as they say. Let's hope you don't land yourself a shark while you're here, hey?'

'I'm keeping well away from the water,' Kitty said.

Gwen looked past Kitty and smiled. 'Ah, speak of the devil,' she said. 'Jake, I believe you've already met our new doctor—Kitty Cargill from London?'

'Sure did,' Jake said with an easy smile. 'Did she tell you she was dressed like a hooker at the time?'

Kitty threw him a furious little glare before turning to Gwen. 'I was at a fancy dress party with my cousin,' she explained. 'I thought she'd broken her ankle, and since this was the closest emergency department I brought her in here. But I dearly wish I hadn't, because it's clear that Dr Chandler thinks it's highly amusing to embarrass me about it at every available opportunity.'

'Bad Jake,' Gwen remonstrated playfully. 'Leave the poor girl alone.' The buzzer rang at the front desk. 'That's my break over. Hope you settle in well, Dr Cargill. Call me if you need anything. Bye.'

Kitty was still fuming. 'Is there anyone in the hospital you *haven't* told?' she asked. 'What about the cleaners and cooks and orderlies? Maybe you could release the CCTV footage. That would be quite hilarious, don't you think?'

'Now, why didn't I think of that?' Jake said with a gleaming smile.

Kitty reined in her temper with an effort. 'I'd like to put that embarrassing episode behind me,' she said. 'I have to work here in a professional capacity. I don't want patients and staff giggling behind my back every time I come to work.'

'You're very uptight, aren't you?'

Her brows snapped together. 'Pardon me for being a little tense, but right at this minute I'm having trouble figuring out if you are the director of this department or the ringmaster at a circus.'

The silence rang like the one left after the sudden cracking of a stock whip.

'My office,' he said. 'Ten minutes.'

Kitty saw the hint of steel in his dark blue eyes before he strode away. Her stomach gave a nervous little flutter. She hadn't been at work more than an hour. Was she going to be sacked on her very first day?

Jake Chandler's office was down at the end of the unit, next to the ultrasound room. Kitty straightened her shoulders and gave the door a tentative rap.

'Come in,' he commanded.

She stepped into the office and closed the door behind her. 'I'd like to apologise,' she said, clasping and unclasping her sweaty hands. 'I was unpardonably rude to you. I don't know what came over me. It was unprofessional of me. I'm sorry.'

He remained seated behind his desk, his dark blue eyes quietly assessing her as he clicked a ballpoint pen on and off.

Kitty chewed at her lower lip. 'I suppose you think I've got no sense of humour.'

'What I think is you're only apologising because you're afraid you're going to get fired.'

She met his diamond-hard gaze. '*Am* I going to get fired?' she asked.

He gave the pen another few clicks. 'Do you think you deserve to be dismissed?' he asked still nailing her with his gaze.

She quickly moistened her pavement-dry lips. 'It depends.'

'On what?'

'On whether you have a sense of humour.'

He held her challenging look with implacable force. 'Dr Cargill,' he said. 'I would like to make something quite clear right from the outset. I enjoy a joke with the best of them. I don't believe in making an already tense and unpredictable workplace unbearable with autocratic or tyrannical behaviour. Humour is at times a safety valve in a department where life and death walk the same tightrope, to borrow the metaphor you used earlier. But one thing I will not tolerate in any shape or form is outright impertinence—especially from a newly appointed staff member who has not yet completed a full day of work. Do I make myself clear?'

Kitty ground her teeth until her jaw ached. 'Yes, Dr Chandler.'

His bluer-than-blue eyes tussled with hers in a lock that made the silence hum with tension.

A funny fizzing sensation bubbled in her belly as his steely gaze slipped to her mouth. Her lips felt the brush of his gaze as if his lips had physically rested there. It was the strangest feeling—one she had never experienced before. She became aware of her mouth, her skin, her body and her senses in a way she never had previously.

It was disquieting.

It was unsettling.

It was threatening and yet somehow...*alluring...*

Kitty gave herself a mental slap. Jake Chandler was a playboy. She had already been warned about him. He was a heartbreaker, and the last thing she needed was another blow to her confidence by a player, not a stayer.

'May I go now?' she asked.

He gave his pen one last click before tossing it to one side and leaning back in his chair. 'What did you do all weekend?' he asked. 'I didn't see you come out of your house even once.'

'I was unpacking.' *And moping and crying and wallowing in self-pity.*

'The social committee have organised a welcome-to-the-unit thing for all new staff members on Friday night at a bar in Bondi,' he said. 'Gwen will give you the details. It'll be a chance to meet most of the permanent staff.' His lips moved in a tiniest of twitches. 'That is unless you have something or someone else already booked in your diary?'

She gave him a look. 'So far I'm free.'

'So it's a date, then.' He got to his feet and the room instantly shrank to the size of a shoebox.

Kitty tried to ignore the way his commanding presence made her feel so tiny and feminine. She had been an inch taller than Charles. She had worn ballet flats most of the time to compensate. But even in those ridiculous heels the other night Jake Chandler had towered over her.

But it wasn't just his height. Something about him made her feel super-aware and edgy.

He *exuded* raw masculinity.

He was all primal male in the prime of his life. Testosterone pumped through his body like fuel through a Formula One car on full throttle.

Her mind began to drift… How would it feel to have that firm mouth press down on hers? She had never kissed anyone but Charles. Would it feel different? *How* different? What would it feel like to have Jake Chandler's strong, capable hands explore her contours? Her belly gave a little tumble-turn as she thought of his body touching hers, moving against hers…

She blinked herself out of her disturbing little daydream. 'I—I'd best be getting back to work,' she said. 'My shift started ten minutes ago.'

He held her gaze for a moment longer than was necessary. Had he sensed where her mind had been? she wondered. Was that why his eyes were so dark and glittering, and his mouth tilted upwards in that almost-smile?

'I'll see you out there in a couple of hours,' he said, resuming his seat and reaching for the phone on his desk. 'I have a couple of calls to make as well as a management meeting.'

'Why is the patient from Bay Three being sent for a CT?' Jake asked Lei Chung on his way back on the unit.

'Dr Cargill ordered it,' Lei said.

'But it's a straight-out case of appendicitis,' Jake said. 'What else is she hoping to find in there? The crown jewels?'

'She's certainly very thorough,' Lei said. 'You should see the blood-work she's ordered on Mrs Harper in Bay Nine. Pathology's going to be backed up for hours getting through that lot.'

Jake frowned as he made his way to the main A&E office, where he could see Kitty Cargill sitting writing up patient notes. His meeting with hospital management hadn't gone well. Patient work-up times had to go down and more beds were being cut. He had one staff member off sick and another one out on stress leave. There were times when he wondered why he had chosen A&E as a specialty. Right now dermatology was looking pretty damn good.

'Got a minute, Dr Cargill?' he asked.

She looked up from her notes. 'Is it about Mr O'Brien in Bay Four?' she asked, pushing her chair back and rising to her feet. 'I'm waiting to hear back from MRI. They think they can squeeze him in just after lunch.'

'Why are you sending him for an MRI?' Jake asked.

'He's got symptoms of acute sciatica with muscle weakness in one leg,' she said. 'He also complained of bladder frequency. He's probably got nerve compression starting to damage nerve root function, but we need to exclude a spinal tumour.'

'But if you think he's got cord compression why wouldn't you just refer him straight on to neurosurgery?' Jake asked.

Her grey eyes flickered and then hardened. 'I

thought it was important to have an exact diagnosis first,' she said.

'That's not our job here. You're wasting precious time and valuable resources doing other
people's jobs for them,' Jake said. 'We have a
top-notch neurosurgical team at St Benedict's,
headed by Lewis Beck. His registrar is more
than capable of dealing with this while you get
on with assessing the next patient.'

She stood very straight and stiff before him,
her chin set at a haughty height. 'It takes time to
do a proper work-up,' she said. 'I don't believe
in taking shortcuts and handing patients over
half assessed. If my diagnosis is wrong, then it's
wasting the time of other services.'

'Listen—our job is to efficiently assess them,
not find out their star sign,' Jake said. 'While
you're busily documenting their favourite colour
and what their neighbour's dog's name is, another patient is waiting in the back of an ambu-
lance trying to get in here to one of our blocked
beds.'

Her jaw worked for a moment, as if she was

forcibly holding back a stinging retort. 'Will that be all, Dr Chandler?' she said.

Jake felt that stirring in his groin again. Something about Kitty Cargill with her feisty little eye-locks and her stubbornly upthrust chin made him want to back her into the nearest storeroom and steal a kiss from that tempting mouth of hers. He couldn't remember a time when he had felt such a powerful attraction to a woman. The betraying little movements and gestures of her face and body indicated she was just as acutely aware of him as he was of her. He could see it now, in the way her grey gaze kept slipping to his mouth as if she had no control over it. The tip of her tongue sneaked out and swept over her lips as if preparing them for the descent of his.

'It's not in my nature to run this department like a drill sergeant,' he said, forcing himself to focus on her eyes, not her mouth. 'I expect a lot from my team, but I don't ask anything of them I wouldn't be prepared to do myself. I realise it will take time for you to learn the ropes of how things are done here. I'm prepared to give you some leeway while you settle in. We'll assess things in a week or two.'

A little frown appeared over her eyes. 'Are you putting me on some type of probation?' she asked.

'That will be all, Dr Cargill,' Jake said, dismissing her. 'You'd better get back on the ward. There are patients to see.'

Kitty seethed all the way home from the hospital. She had mostly managed to avoid Jake during the rest of her shift. A steady stream of patients had needed attending to, but nothing major that had required her to interact with him directly.

She didn't like the thought of his wait-and-see approach to her appointment. She had got the position on merit and she expected to keep it. What right did he have to question her management of patients? She had been trained by some of London's best. How dared Jake Chandler leave her in such a horrid state of limbo? She had moved all the way across the globe to take this post. He had no right to make her feel insecure and inadequate. She was competent and hardworking. That was the one thing that had carried her through the heartache of the last few months. She might not be the biggest extrovert, or one of those effortlessly glamorous party girls, but she was damn good at her job.

Once she got back to the town house she changed into her one-piece bathing costume and some casual separates and headed straight for the beach. The sting of the sun had eased now it was early evening. The iconic arc of Bondi Beach was still heavily dotted with bodies making the most of the long, hot summer. Dozens of fit-looking surfers were out at the back of the swell, waiting for the perfect wave. Kitty couldn't help envying their agility and grace. She had never been all that confident around water. She could swim…well, maybe that was stretching it a teensy bit. She could get from one end of a very short pool to the other. The ocean was another thing entirely. She had been to the beach plenty of times, but gentle, bay-like ones—ones with shingle or pebbles, not sand as fine as sugar and a swell that was rolling in with a roar that sounded like thunder as each wave crashed against the shore.

Kitty laid out her towel on the sand, anchoring the four corners with each of her flip-flops and two shells. She carefully tucked her keys inside her hat, along with her sunglasses, before she walked down to the water's edge between the lifesaver patrol flags.

The water was warmer than she was used to and yet refreshing as she let it froth over her ankles and shins. She went in up to her knees and stood there watching as children half her height went out further, shrieking and squealing in delight as they jumped over or dived under the waves.

The lowering sun was like a warm caress on her back and shoulders, easing some of the tight golf ball-sized knots that had gathered there.

'Watch me, Uncle Jake!' A young boy's voice rang out over the sound of the surf.

Kitty felt the hairs on the back of her neck stand up and the golf balls in her shoulders knock together.

How many Jakes were there *in* Sydney and *at* Bondi Beach on *this* particular evening?

She looked to her right and saw Jake Chandler—*the Jake Chandler*—standing watching as a young boy bodysurfed a small wave.

Her heart tripped.

Her belly hollowed.

Her mouth watered.

Jake was standing less than a metre away from her. He was naked from the waist up. He was wet. He was tanned. He was lean. He was muscular in all the right places.

*He was gorgeous.*

'Why is that lady staring at you, Uncle Jake?'

Kitty blinked herself out of her stasis, embarrassed colour shooting to her face as Jake's blue gaze turned and met hers. 'I'm not staring…' she said, and stared.

Jake's thick dark lashes were spiky with seawater. He had a lazy smile playing about his mouth. He had a day's growth of sexy stubble. His black hair was wet. His shoulders were broad, his hips narrow. His abdomen washboard-flat, his groin—

Kitty swallowed and blushed some more as she dragged her gaze back to his. 'I didn't know you were an uncle,' she said, in a paltry effort to cover her mortification.

Jake put his hand on his nephew's wiry shoulder. 'Nathan,' he said. 'I'd like you to meet a new member of my staff at the hospital. This is Dr Cargill.'

Kitty smiled at the child, who looked about nine or ten years old. 'Hi. I'm pleased to meet you, Nathan.'

'You talk funny,' Nathan said, screwing up his face.

'It's called the Queen's English, Nate,' Jake said. 'You'd do well to learn it—and some manners while you're at it.'

The boy wriggled out from under Jake's hand. 'Can I surf some more?' he asked.

'Yeah, but stay between the flags,' Jake said. He turned and looked at Kitty again. 'Sorry about that. He's a good kid but he needs a bit of polish.'

Kitty tried not to stare at those long spiky eyelashes. 'He's very like you,' she said.

His brow came up in a sardonic arc. 'You think I need a bit of a polish too, do you, Dr Cargill?'

She felt her cheeks burn as she fought to hold his gaze. 'That's not what I meant at all,' she said, with as much composure as she could muster whilst standing partially naked before him. 'I meant you're like him in looks. Your eyes, your hair—that sort of thing.'

Jake returned his gaze to the waves, where his nephew was bodysurfing with varying degrees of success. 'He's a handful,' he said. 'I try and wear him out for my sister Rosie.' He glanced at her again. 'That's whose party it was the other night. As a single mum she doesn't get to kick up her heels much.'

'Oh.' Kitty caught her bottom lip with her teeth.

'Nathan's father shot through before he was born.'

'I'm sorry…'

'She's not,' Jake said, swinging his gaze back to hers. 'She's better off without him.'

She tugged at her lip some more. 'I mean I'm sorry about complaining about the music the

other night,' she said. 'It must have seemed so…
so petty.'

He checked on his nephew again before turning his gaze back to her. 'You don't like being
out of your depth, do you?' he asked.

'What makes you say that?'

'You're only wet up to your knees,' he said.
'We usually have to drag overseas tourists unconscious from this beach. A lot of them dive in
without checking the conditions first.'

'I don't like leaping before I look,' she said.

'Can you swim?'

Kitty flashed him an affronted look. 'Of
course I can swim.'

'Give me a shout if you need a hand with some
stroke correction,' he said.

'No doubt breaststroke is *your* particular specialty?' she said with an arch look.

His lips curved upwards in a sexy smile, but
not before his glinting eyes had dipped to the
hint of her cleavage first. 'How'd you guess?' he
said, and then before she could think of a return
he had joined his nephew in the rushing waves.

# CHAPTER THREE

KITTY went back to her towel. Resting her chin on her bent knees, she concentrated on watching the surfers further out, but her gaze kept drifting back to where Jake was coaching his nephew. He looked so magnificently male, so vital and fit and healthy. She couldn't help thinking of Charles, with his fair skin, his slight paunch and his receding hairline.

She pulled her thoughts back into line. She wasn't the shallow looks-are-everything type. She was attracted to depth of character, to strong values and dedication and ambition, to caring for others…

She chewed at her lip as she watched Jake scoop his nephew out of a particularly rough wave, holding him steady against him until Nathan got his breath back and found his feet.

*He would make a wonderful father.*

Kitty felt ambushed by the errant thought. What did she care what sort of father he would make? It had nothing to do with her. What right did her belly have to give a soft little flutter at the thought of him holding a tiny baby in his large masculine hands?

She got to her feet and shook the sand off her towel, frowning as she folded it into a neat square. It might be close to seven-thirty in the evening but she'd clearly had way too much sun.

'Leaving already?' Jake asked as he came towards her across the sand.

Kitty drank in the sight of him. How could anyone look *that* good after a twelve-hour day at work and an hour of kid-sitting at the beach? 'I—I have to wash my hair,' she said, flustered, putting a hand to her hair.

'You didn't even get it wet,' he said.

She ignored his comment and looked past him. 'Where's your nephew?' she asked.

'My sister collected him a few minutes ago,' he said. 'I would've introduced you to her but she was in a hurry.'

Kitty hugged her towel against her chest as if

that would stop her heart from beating so erratically and so fast. His skin glistened with droplets of water, and she watched in spellbound fascination as they rolled like a row of glittering diamonds down over his muscled chest. He smelt of the sea, with a grace note of something else—perhaps a lingering trace of his citrus aftershave or shampoo.

He was standing close enough for her to feel a tiny shower of water drops land on her skin when he finger-combed his hair back off his face. She didn't understand how such a sensation could have a disturbing undercurrent of intimacy about it, but it did. Her skin shivered as if he had slowly run his long tanned fingers down the slim length of her bare arms. She moistened her lips and tried to get her brain to work.

'I have to get going…' she said, but her feet didn't move. It felt as if the sand had suddenly turned into quick-setting concrete.

'I'll go in with you if you like,' he said, nodding towards the ocean. 'Just till you get your confidence. Your first time can be a bit scary.'

Kitty's breath stalled. It was tempting. It was

hot, and the water felt marvellous around her knees, but what if he *touched* her? What if those strongly muscled arms actually *held* her? 'You don't have to babysit me,' she said with icy hauteur. 'I'm perfectly able to take care of myself.'

He took the towel she was holding like a lifeline and tossed it to the sand at their feet, his dark blue eyes never once leaving hers. 'Prove it,' he said.

Kitty put her shoulders back and her chin up. 'All right,' she said, and spun around and made her way to the water. She splashed through the waves until she was in up to her waist before she turned to look at him. But he wasn't watching from the beach. He had followed her in. He was less than half a metre away. Did he think she was *that* hopeless?

She gritted her teeth.

*She would show him.*

'Watch out!' he said suddenly.

Kitty turned just as a bigger than normal wave smashed into her. She felt as if she had been thrown into a washing machine on a rapid wash cycle. She couldn't see. She couldn't breathe. She couldn't stand up even if she had known which way was up.

Suddenly a strong hand gripped one of her arms and hauled her upright. She blinked the briny water out of her stinging eyes and looked up at Jake's face. Her body was pressed against the rock-like wall of his by the force of the water. Every hard plane of his body was imprinted on her softer ones. Her breasts were pushed up against his chest, her belly against his washboard abdomen. One of his arms was like a band of iron behind her back; the other was holding her hand in an equally firm grip, his long fingers entwined with hers. His strong legs were slightly apart to brace against the undertow of the water, and the cradle of his pelvis against hers reminded her shockingly, alarmingly, *deliciously* of all that was different between them.

She felt a flickering between her thighs, like a thousand tiny wings beating inside a cramped space. Electricity shot through her veins, sending sparks of reaction up and down her spine, through every limb, even to the very ends of her fizzing fingertips and her curling toes.

Her eyes went to his mouth. She couldn't stop staring at the rough stubble that surrounded it. The desire to reach up and trace that sexy masculine regrowth with her fingertips was almost overwhelming. Her hands were splayed against the hard wall of his chest, and that electrifying sensation was passing from his body to hers through the sensitive pads of her fingers. She could feel the thudding of his heartbeat drumming into her palm.

She couldn't remember the last time she had been this close to a man… Well, she could, but that final goodbye hug from Charles hadn't felt anything like this.

'You're way out of your depth,' Jake said, with an unreadable expression on his face.

Kitty couldn't get her breathing to steady, but it had very little to do with the water she'd inadvertently swallowed. 'A little…perhaps…'

He braced her against him as another wave bore down on them. 'Hold on,' he said.

The crazy water swished and swirled around them but Kitty barely noticed. She was acutely aware of his body pressed against hers, from her soft breasts to his hard chest, from her smooth slim legs to his strong hair-roughened thighs. She felt the imprint of his arousal against her belly. That starkly primal instinctive reaction of male to female sent her senses into a madcap frenzy. His body seemed to thicken and harden as each heart-stopping second passed. She felt his heartbeat pick up under her hand. It was just a hint of escalation, but it relayed a message that was older than time itself.

Their gazes locked for a moment.

The sound of the ocean and people bathing around them faded. It was like being in a vacuum where no one else existed.

It was just the two of them: a man and a woman, male and female—*alone*.

Jake's gaze slipped to her mouth, those dark blue eyes perusing it for long pulsing seconds as if memorising every tiny crease and line of her lips. 'Time to get you out of danger,' he said, blinking a couple of times. 'You don't want to get dumped unexpectedly again.'

Kitty ran her tongue over her mouth, tasting the ocean and a need so strong she felt it tingling under the surface of her lips. 'I thought it was supposed to be safe between the flags,' she said.

'It depends,' he said as he led her by the hand to shallower water.

She flicked her wet hair back over her shoulders and glanced at him as she sloshed through the lace-like foam of the shallows, trying not to notice how his fingers were so warm and strong where they were curled around hers. 'On what?'

'On whether you can handle the conditions,' he said, releasing her hand once she was steady on her feet. 'Swimming in a pool is not the same as swimming in the ocean. Every day at the beach is different. You never know when a bigger than normal wave is going to come unless you have experience at reading the swell.'

'Maybe I'll stick to the paddling pool for the time being,' she said. 'At least there are no sharks there.'

His dark blue eyes glinted down at her. 'I think you'll be fine once you gain your confidence,' he said. 'In no time at all you'll be riding those waves like the best of them.'

Kitty had a feeling he wasn't talking just about

the ocean. But she wasn't sure if he was talking about gaining confidence at work or in her private life. Was he warning her about getting involved with him? Letting her know the rules from the outset? Her instincts warned her that a relationship with him would not be a safe but boring mechanical lapping of a municipal pool. It would be diving head-first into a surging tide of deep rushing water that carried a constant threat of imminent danger.

*She'd be best to stay well clear of it.*

She reached for her towel and wrapped herself in it even though she wasn't in the least bit cold. In fact she felt hot, both inside and out. Her skin still tingled and fizzed where he had touched her. And those tiny wings were still beating a soft but insistent rhythm deep inside her every time his eyes met hers, with that ancient primal message of male and female attraction virtually impossible to ignore.

*Like right now.*

Kitty suppressed a shiver as those blue eyes— as dark and deep as the ocean that surged and pulsed behind him—held hers.

The raw energy of his body reached out in invisible waves to wash over her, mesmerising her, tantalising her, consuming her. She felt the magnetic force-field of his tall masculine frame standing in front of her.

If she took a step forward she would be able to touch him. The temptation to do so was almost overwhelming. She wanted to place her hands on that muscular chest, to slide her palms over that damp hot skin, to feel those hard planes and contours, to look up and see the answering attraction in his eyes. But somehow she scrunched her fingers into her palms and stepped back instead.

'I have to get going...' she said, and almost tripped over her own feet in the loose sand in her haste to escape.

One of his hands shot out and steadied her, his fingers wrapping around her wrist like a steel bracelet. 'Careful,' he said.

Kitty swallowed as she glanced down at his fingers overlapping each other on the slender bones of her wrist. They looked so exotic and dark against the creamy paleness of her skin. Her pulse hammered beneath his touch. It felt as if a hummingbird was trapped inside her veins. She wondered if he could feel it. Was that why he had not let her go even though she was no longer in any danger of tripping?

She gave him a sheepish look. 'You can let me go now.'

He slowly unwound his fingers, his eyes still meshed with hers. 'I guess I'll see you around,' he said.

'Yes, I expect so,' Kitty said. She waited a beat before adding, 'Thank you for the...rescue.'

He flashed a brief on-off smile. 'You're welcome.'

And without another word he ambled off to where he had left his towel further along the beach, turning every female head as he went.

Kitty slowly released a breath and only just resisted the urge to fan her face with one of her hands. 'Way too much sun, my girl,' she said under her breath and, trudging through the sand, headed home.

As soon as Jake walked into the A&E unit the next morning Gwen and a nurse and a resident who were in the office went silent, just as if someone had flicked a volume switch to mute.

'What's going on?' he asked.

'I have to check some bloods,' the resident said, and dashed out.

'Er…me too,' the nurse said, and quickly followed the resident.

Jake eyeballed Gwen. 'What gives?' he asked.

'You were seen canoodling with Dr Cargill,' Gwen said as she folded her arms across her ample chest. 'Apparently it's all over the hospital.'

Jake frowned. 'Canoodling?'

'Yes,' Gwen said in mild reproach. 'I thought you liked to keep your private life separate from your professional one—or are you making a special exception this time?'

*'Canoodling?'* he said again. 'What the hell is that supposed to mean?'

'You know exactly what it means,' Gwen said. 'What are you thinking, Jake? You know how awkward it gets when staff members have flings with each other. It's bad enough when they work in separate departments, but on the same unit? Everyone feels the fall-out when it's bye-bye time.'

'I am not involved with Dr Cargill,' he said. *Yet*, he tacked on silently. 'Who the hell put that rumour out there?'

'You work together,' Gwen said. 'Word has it you live in the same town house block, and now we hear you're playing together.'

He looked at her blankly. 'Playing together?'

Gwen gave him a look. 'On the beach,' she said. 'In full view of everyone.'

Jake barked out a laugh. 'I was teaching her to swim…or sort of.'

Gwen rolled her eyes. 'Well, whatever you were doing with her has been witnessed and reported. I thought you should know.'

'Thanks a bunch,' Jake said, grinning. 'Does Dr Cargill know we are now an item?'

'Not yet,' Gwen said with grim foreboding. 'But I hope I'm not around when she finds out.'

# CHAPTER FOUR

KITTY was examining a patient with a mild blunt force trauma to his forehead in Cubicle Four when she overheard two junior nurses talking as they changed the linen in cubicle three.

'Talk about a fast worker,' one of them said. 'She's only been here a day or two and she's already got her hooks into him.'

'Yeah, well, she certainly got his attention by turning up in that hooker costume the other night,' the other one said. 'Do you reckon it was staged?'

'Must've been,' the other one said. 'What a slut.'

Kitty's heart slammed into her breastbone. She broke out in a sweat, her cheeks firing up and her skin prickling all over in outrage.

'Is everything all right?' the patient lying on

the bed asked worriedly. 'I'm not going to die, am I?'

Kitty forced a cool professional smile to her stiff features. 'No, Mr Jenkins,' she said. 'You have a small haematoma that will take a day or two to subside. The skin isn't broken, so there's a slim to none chance of infection. You're not showing any signs of a concussion, but you need to take things easy over the next day or so. Don't drive, operate heavy machinery or consume alcohol for the next twenty-four hours.'

'Thanks, Doctor,' the man said. 'The wife will kill me if I cark it now. We've got a cruise booked for next month. We've been saving up for it for five years.'

'You'll be fine by then,' Kitty said, patting his arm before she left the cubicle.

During her lunch break Kitty went in search of Jake Chandler, but he wasn't on the floor or in either of the doctors' rooms. He was in his office. She felt every eye following her as she made her way through the unit. She had been the subject of hospital gossip before. Her break-up with Charles had done the rounds. It had been excruciating to know everyone was talking about her private life in such lurid detail. She had felt so exposed; so raw and vulnerable. She knew it would only have got worse after Charles's wedding so she had decided to take herself out of the picture. But it seemed that even on the other side of the world people with pathetically small lives thought it sport to speculate on the lives of others. She didn't have the option of running away this time. She would have to face it and deal with it.

She took a calming breath and rapped firmly on the door.

'Come in, Dr Cargill.'

Kitty's hand stilled where it rested on the doorknob. So he had been expecting her, had he? What was he playing at? Was this his idea of a joke? Did he have nothing better to do than make a laughing-stock out of her?

She pulled her shoulders back and kept her chin up, and turned the knob and entered the office, closing the door with a resounding click behind her. 'I hate to interrupt you when you're busy, but—'

'It's all right,' he said. 'I've ordered the invitations, and I know a really cool florist who'll do the flowers for mate's rates, not retail.'

Kitty blinked. 'Pardon?'

'The wedding,' he said indolently, swivelling his office chair from side to side.

'Wedding?' She frowned until her forehead ached. 'What wedding?'

His blue eyes shone with amusement. 'Ours,' he said. 'Apparently we're engaged and expecting triplets.'

She felt her jaw drop. 'Are you out of your mind?'

He smiled a breath-stealing smile. 'Gossip,' he said. 'You only have to look at someone around here and people start planning the guest list for the wedding.'

Kitty opened and closed her mouth, totally lost for words.

'Apparently we were caught canoodling,' he said.

'Canoodling?'

He gave her a been-there-asked-that look.

'Yeah,' he said. 'I looked it up in the dictionary. It means to kiss and cuddle amorously.'

'But we didn't do any such thing!' she blurted.

He lifted one of his broad shoulders up and down in a casual shrug. 'Doesn't matter,' he said. 'It looked like it. That's enough to set the tongues wagging around here. No one believes me when I tell them I was actually saving your life.'

'You weren't saving my life,' she said, sending him an affronted glare. 'I wasn't drowning.'

'And I wasn't kissing and cuddling you amorously, but there you go,' he said. 'What's done is done.'

Kitty clenched her fists by her sides. 'Then it will have to be undone,' she insisted. 'I don't want people speculating on my private life.'

'Relax,' he said. 'They'll find someone else to talk about soon enough.'

She strode over and slammed her hands on the desk in front of him, leaning forward to drive home her point. 'Relax?' she said. 'How can I relax? I heard two nurses talking about me in the next cubicle while I was with a patient. I was totally mortified. They called me a slut. They said I'd staged it the night I brought my cousin into A&E just to get your attention.'

His eyes took their merry time meeting hers, taking a sensual detour to the shadow of her cleavage, which she had inadvertently exposed to him. She quickly straightened, but it was too late. She could see the gleam of male appraisal in the depths of his dark blue gaze as it met with hers. The temperature of her skin went up to blistering hot and a hollow feeling opened up in her stomach.

'I'll have a word with them and put them straight,' he said. 'And if I hear any further gossip I'll categorically deny we have anything going on.'

'Thank you,' she said, pressing her lips together for a moment. 'I would appreciate it.'

He leaned back in his chair with a squeak of vinyl. 'Just for the record, Dr Cargill,' he said. 'Next time you come in here you'd better not close the door.'

'Pardon?'

He nodded towards the door behind her which

she had clicked shut on her entry. 'You know how people's minds work,' he said. 'A man and a woman in an office together behind a closed door... Who knows what they might get up to.'

Kitty's cheeks exploded with colour. 'That might be how other people's minds work but it's certainly not the way mine operates,' she said.

A lazy smile lurked around the edges of his mouth. 'Good for you,' he said. 'Nice to know there's still some innocence in this big, bad old world of ours.'

She narrowed her eyes at him. 'You think I'm naive and inexperienced, don't you?' she asked.

He pushed back his chair and sauntered over to the office door, standing with a hand on the doorknob without turning it. 'I think, Dr Cargill,' he said, 'that you should get back to work before someone comes looking for you. We don't want any more gossip circulating about us, do we?'

Kitty snatched in a quick unsteady breath. She could smell his clean citrus and wood smell. She could see the individual pinpricks of his cleanly shaven jaw. She could see the sensual contours of his sinfully tempting mouth. She could see the flare of those ink-black pupils in the dark blue sea of his eyes. She was barely aware of sending her tongue out to moisten her lips until she saw those sapphire-blue eyes drop to her mouth to track the movement.

Something tightened in the air.

It was an invisible energy, a force Kitty could feel passing over the entire surface of her skin, disrupting the nerves inside and out, making them super-aware and super-sensitive.

She became aware of the deep thudding of her heart: a *boom, boom, boom* sensation inside her ribcage that was almost audible.

His eyes moved from her mouth to mesh with hers in a heart-stopping little lockdown that sent her senses into a tailspin. 'You know, there is an alternative to handling this situation we find ourselves in,' he said, in a deep and husky tone that sent a shower of reaction down her spine.

'Th-there is?' she said in an equally raspy voice.

His eyes went to her mouth again, resting there an infinitesimal moment before meeting her eyes once more. 'Instead of denying it we could say it's true,' he said. 'Then everyone will stop speculating about us.'

Kitty blinked. 'But…but it's not true.'

One side of his mouth tilted. 'I know, but only we would know that.'

She frowned. 'So you're saying we should *pretend* we're having a fling just to stop people gossiping about us?' she asked.

'It could work,' he said. 'It'll stop the "are they?" or "aren't they?" comments.'

Kitty made a little scoffing sound. 'But you're not my type. I would never in a million years date someone like you.'

'Same goes.'

She pursed her lips as she considered his comeback. Why wouldn't he date someone like her? What was wrong with her?

Wasn't she pretty enough?

Smart enough?

*Too* smart?

'I can imagine I don't quite fit the stereotype for your usual bedmate,' she said. 'A brain is not essential—only a pulse, right?'

He gave her one of his lazy smiles. 'It has to be a strong, healthy pulse,' he said. 'Great stamina is required when sleeping with me.'

Kitty could have cooked a raw egg on both cheeks. 'I am *not* sleeping with you, Dr Chandler,' she said. 'Not in pretence or in reality.'

He opened the door for her with exaggerated gallantry. 'Then it's best if we keep our distance, don't you think?'

She put her chin up. 'That's exactly what I intend to do,' she said, and stalked out.

Jake was about to leave his office for a meeting when his mobile rang. He glanced at the caller ID on the screen and muttered a swearword under his breath before he answered it. 'You'd better have a good excuse for not showing up for Rosie's birthday,' he said to his younger brother.

'When was it her birthday?' Robbie asked.

Jake rolled his eyes. 'Why haven't you returned any of my calls or texts?'

'I ran out of credit on my phone.'

'What? Again?' Jake asked. 'I gave you heaps of credit only a fortnight ago.'

'Yeah, well, I had to make a lot of calls,' Robbie said in a surly tone.

'What a pity one of them wasn't to one of your sisters or to me,' Jake muttered.

'Get off my case, Jake, you're not my father.'

Jake pinched the bridge of his nose to clear the red mist of anger that appeared before his eyes. 'No, I'm damn well not,' he said. 'You know, I never thought I'd say this, but I'm glad Mum didn't survive that car accident. It would've broken her heart to see you stuff your life up like this. What were you thinking, Robbie? This time two years ago you were halfway through your engineering degree. Now you're living on the streets.'

'I'm not living on the streets,' Robbie said. 'I've got mates I'm hanging with.'

'You know what they say about lying down with stray dogs,' Jake said. 'Sooner or later you're going to get fleas.'

'You're just pissed because I'm out having fun and you're not,' Robbie said.

'You call getting hammered or stoned every night *fun*?' Jake said, anger and frustration making his throat tight and his voice hoarse. 'Where's the fun in getting Hep C or AIDS from a dirty needle, huh? Tell me that. Tell me what's fun about wrecking your life and everyone else's in the process.'

'I'm not using any more,' Robbie said. 'I'm clean, man.'

Jake was holding his phone so tightly he thought the screen was going to crack. How could he trust a word that Robbie said? Sometimes it felt as if someone had hijacked his little brother's body. It was Robbie on the outside, but it wasn't his kid brother on the inside. Where had that sunny faced, happy-go-lucky kid gone? Where was the boy he had coached through the turbulent years of adolescence in the absence of their deadbeat father, who hadn't even stayed around long enough to see Robbie born? Where was the pimply teenager he had taught to drive? Where was the young man who'd used to drop in to his flat at least three times a week just to hang out after lectures? Who'd talked to him late into the night of his hopes and dreams and aspirations? Who had looked up to him not just as an older brother, but also as a mentor?

*And, even more heart wrenching, would Jake ever be able to get him back?*

He pinched the bridge of his nose again, taking a calming breath before he spoke. 'Tell me where you are and I'll come and get you,' he said. 'You can stay with me for a few days. We'll sort something out.'

'I don't need a place to stay,' Robbie said. 'I just need some cash.'

Jake dropped his hand from his face. 'You know what I feel about handing you money, Robbie. If you need food I'll buy it. If you need rent paid I'll pay it. But don't ask me to hand you money to pay for drink or drugs. I can't do that. I *won't* do that.'

The phone went dead.

Jake put the phone back on the desk and dragged his hand over his face. Was this nightmare ever going to end? Where had he gone wrong? He had thought it bad enough when Rosie had got herself pregnant by that jerk who had left her stranded at the age of nineteen. But that was nothing compared to this. Robbie was hellbent on self-destruction and there wasn't a thing he or anyone could do to stop it.

All the sacrifices he had made to keep his family together were *still* not enough. All the opportunities he could have taken he had gladly relinquished, just to see his siblings make their way in the world. He had curtailed many of his own plans to make sure his siblings got the care and the resources they needed. The girls were finally on their feet now. And he had been so proud that Robbie had decided to go to university—thrilled that all the hopes their mother had had for each of her children were finally coming to fruition. He had thought when Robbie was doing well in his studies that things would be smooth sailing from then on. But just when he had thought it was safe to have a life of his own, free of the responsibilities he had shouldered for so long, everything had come crashing down.

What more could he do? Did he have to spend the rest of his life worrying about his brother? Was Robbie ever going to grow out of this stage and be responsible for himself? Or was this how it was going to be for ever?

'What's this I hear about you getting it on with the new recruit in A&E?' asked Greg Hickey, one of the orthopaedic surgeons, in the doctors' room later that day.

Jake put his teaspoon down on the sink. 'Just a rumour, Greg,' he said. 'You know what this place is like. You only have to look at someone and everyone thinks you're sleeping with them.'

Greg gave him a cynical grin. 'That's because you usually are.'

Jake gave a dismissive shrug. 'She's not my type.'

'She's a London girl, isn't she?' Greg asked as he poured himself a coffee from the brew on the hotplate.

'Yeah,' Jake said, thinking of Kitty's cute little accent and the way she put her nose in the air when she wanted to make a point.

'And quite pretty, so I've been told,' Greg added.

Jake took a sip of his coffee as he thought

about the heart-shaped face and the stormy grey eyes that had stared him down across his desk earlier that day. His body had leapt to attention. He had felt so tempted to come around from behind his desk and taste the temptation of her full mouth. Was it really as soft as it looked? She wasn't the lipstick type, but she wore a shimmery lip gloss that made her lips look luscious. Would they taste of vanilla or strawberries?

Her hair had been pulled back in a tight, schoolmarmish knot at the back of her head. He had wanted to release it from its prim confines and let it cascade freely around her shoulders. He had wanted to run his fingers through it to see if it was as silky as it looked. He couldn't quite rid his mind of imagining her cloud of hair spread out over the pillows on his bed, her slim, creamy limbs entwined with his. Would she be a kitten or a tigress in bed? He got hard just thinking about it. He couldn't rid his mind of her fragrance, either. She had smelled of frangipanis this time, an exotic and alluring scent that had lingered in his office for hours.

'She's all right, I guess,' he said, with another casual up-and-down movement of his shoulders.

Greg chuckled as he reached for the artificial sweetener on the counter. 'You've got it bad, Jakey boy,' he said. 'I can see all the signs.'

'What d'you mean?' Jake asked, frowning. 'What signs?'

'Every time I mentioned her just then you got this goofy sort of dreamy look on your face,' Greg said, leaning back against the counter. 'I reckon you're falling for her.'

Jake gave an uncomfortable laugh. 'You're crazy. I've never fallen for anyone in my life and I'm not going to start now.'

Greg kept grinning. 'Gotta be a first time for everything, right?'

'Wrong,' Jake said, putting his mug down on the table with a little *thwack*. 'Kitty Cargill's far too conservative for me. She doesn't have a funny bone in her body. She's prim and proper and she sweats over the small stuff all the time. She doesn't smile—she glowers. Besides, she's still hankering over some guy who broke her heart back in the home country. I don't think she's here to advance her career at all. She's running away from her failed love-life. I don't need any lame ducks on my staff; God knows it's hard enough to keep everyone's morale up as it is with all these wretched cutbacks. I don't want to have to babysit someone who isn't up to the task.'

'What? You don't think she's competent?' Greg asked, frowning over the rim of his coffee cup.

Jake released a breath and rubbed at the tight muscles at the back of his neck. Maybe he'd laid it on a bit strong. It wouldn't do to sound *too* defensive. 'No, I'm not saying that. She's conscientious—a little too much so if anything. She's eager to learn and the patients like her. She'll find her feet soon enough.'

'Might be just what she needs to boost her confidence,' Greg said. 'A meaningless affair with a man she won't think twice about leaving when it's time to say goodbye.'

'I'm not putting my hand up for the job just yet,' Jake said. 'Not unless I hand over a thousand bucks to one of my sisters.'

'What do you mean?'

'I made a bet with her over Christmas dinner,' Jake said. 'No sex for three months.'

Greg's brows rose. 'So how's that working out for you?'

Jake gave him a rueful look as he shouldered open the door. 'Let's put it this way,' he said. 'I'm spending a whole lot more time at the gym.'

# CHAPTER FIVE

JAKE was on his way back to his town house after a heavy session at the gym when he saw Kitty in the car park, washing a car that had seen better days. She was wearing a pair of shorts that ended at mid-thigh and a loose-fitting T-shirt. Her hair was up in a high ponytail, swinging from side to side as she rubbed the soapy sponge over the duco of her four-cylinder vehicle. She looked young and nubile and so sexy he felt a surge of lust go through him like a rocket blast. Her small but perfect breasts were outlined behind the clingy dampness of her T-shirt, and every time she bent over he caught a delectable glimpse of her creamy flesh. She was humming to herself—a tune he was familiar with but couldn't quite place. She had a hose in her other hand and it was spraying water all over the concrete, running in wasteful rivulets down the storm water drain.

'I hate to take on the role of the fun police but you can't do that around here,' he said.

She jumped and turned around so quickly the high-pressure hose in her hand shot him straight in the groin with a blast of cold water.

He let out a stiff curse as he stepped out of the line of fire. 'What the hell?'

'Sorry,' she said, pointing the hose at the ground, where it sprayed water all over the concrete at her feet. 'I didn't hear you. You scared the wits out of me, coming from nowhere like that.'

He frowned in irritation as he brushed off what water he could from his sodden gym shorts. 'Will you turn off the damn hose, for God's sake?'

She gave her head a little toss that sent her ponytail swinging again. 'I'm washing my new car.'

'You can't use a hose to do that.'

'Why ever not?' she asked, looking at him defiantly. 'How else am I supposed to wash it? Lick it clean?'

Jake looked at her mouth—a habit of his just lately that he couldn't seem to break. He could think of places he would much rather have her lick with her tongue than the dusty duco of her second-hand bomb. 'We have water restrictions here,' he said. 'You can't use a hose to water the garden or wash your car during summer. You have to use a bucket. If you get caught there are hefty fines.'

'Oh…' She looked at the running hose and bit down on her lip. 'I didn't realise.'

Jake moved over to turn the hose off at the tap, asking over his shoulder. 'Where did you get the car?'

Her chin came up a fraction. 'I bought it.'

He came over and ran a hand over the dented paintwork of the front fender. 'How much did you pay for it?' he asked.

She pursed her lips for a tiny heartbeat. 'It wasn't expensive,' she said. 'I didn't want to spend a fortune because I'm only going to be using it for three months.'

'Let's hope it lasts that long,' Jake said, kicking one of the threadbare tyres with his right foot.

'I'm sure it's perfectly fine,' she said, with a little flash of her grey gaze.

'Did you take it for a test drive?'

Her eyes flickered a little, as if something behind them had come loose. 'I drove it around the block at the owner's house and then back to here,' she said. 'It ran smoothly enough.'

Jake grunted. 'Good luck on restarting it.'

Her lips went tight again. 'I'm sure it will start first go,' she said. 'It's only had one owner.'

'How many clicks on the clock?'

A little frown pulled at her brow. 'Clicks?'

'Kilometres.'

'Oh…' She nibbled at her lip again and stepped past him to peer through the driver's window. 'Forty-two thousand.'

Jake rolled his eyes. 'Make that *two hundred* and forty-two thousand—maybe even more.'

She frowned at him again. 'What do you mean?'

'That model is ten years old,' he said. 'Even a little old lady only driving to church on Sundays would've clicked up more than that. You've been sold a lemon, Dr Cargill. Someone's turned the clock back on it for sure.'

She shifted her eyes from his to the car and back again. 'I suppose you think I'm gullible,' she said with a hint of defiance.

'Have you ever bought a car before?' Jake asked.

'I…' Her slim throat rose and fell as she swallowed. 'I used to share one. I lived close to the hospital in London so I didn't really need one of my own.'

Jake gave the windscreen wipers a quick inspection. 'These need replacing,' he said, dusting his hands on his shorts. 'I can get a new set of rubbers for you from a mate of mine. He owns an auto parts shop.'

'I wouldn't want to put you or your friend to any bother,' she said, looking resentful and yet vulnerable and adorably cute all at the same time.

'It's no trouble,' Jake said. 'You'll need new tyres soon too. That rear one is practically bald.'

She worked at her bottom lip again with her

teeth, looking at the car with a defeated look on her expressive heart-shaped face.

'Don't worry,' Jake said. 'I'm sure it'll get you to the hospital and back all right. But I wouldn't take it on any long journeys until you've had it checked by a mechanic. I can give you the name of one who'll take care of it for you without ripping you off.'

'Thank you…' She tucked a strand of hair behind her ear in a discomfited gesture.

'I'll get you a bucket,' he said. 'I have one in my garage.'

'Please don't bother,' she said.

'It's no bother.' Jake walked towards his garage and, fishing his remote out of his shorts pocket, activated the roller door. He ducked his head as the door was rising and grabbed the bucket next to his toolbox. 'Can't leave a job half done, now, can we?' he said as he took the bucket over to the tap and filled it.

'What are you doing?' she asked.

Jake took the sponge from her hand, watching as her eyes flared when his fingers brushed against hers. 'Stand back,' he said with a lop-sided smile. 'This is no job for a lady.'

'I'm not sure what gives you the impression I'm completely rubbish at taking care of the sim-plest tasks,' she said, bristling like a pedigree Persian cat in front of a scruffy mongrel dog. 'But I'll have you know I can wash a car all by myself.'

Jake moved past her stiff little body to soap up the bonnet of the car. 'It won't take a min-ute,' he said. 'You're too short to reach the roof in any case.'

She stood back with her arms folded crossly, her plump mouth pushed forward in a pout. 'That's why I was using the hose,' she said, shooting him a look.

'Yeah, well, don't blame the drought on me,' Jake said, bending over to re-soap the sponge. 'I suppose you don't have to wash cars in England.'

'Why do you say that?' she asked.

'Doesn't it rain all the time?' he asked as he cleaned the rooftop of the car.

'Not *all* the time,' she said, with a hint of de-fensiveness.

A little silence passed.

'Have you been to Britain?' she asked.

Jake squatted down to soap up the rim of the nearest tyre. He thought of the ticket to London he'd had to cancel when he'd found out about Rosie's pregnancy. He'd only planned to go for a couple of months the year after he'd finished medical school. He'd organised for Robbie to stay with a reliable family and the girls with friends. He had counted the days until his first real holiday free of responsibility. But when Rosie had tearfully confessed her predicament he had cancelled his trip and had never got around to booking another.

'It's on my list of things to do.'

'Have you been to Europe?'

'Not yet.'

'Why not?' she asked. 'I thought a man like you would have gone far and wide to sow your wild oats.'

Jake straightened and tossed the sponge in the bucket like a basketball player landing a game-winning shot. 'It hasn't been a priority,' he said. 'Australia's plenty big enough and exciting enough for me.'

'That's rather parochial of you, don't you think?' she said.

He shrugged. 'I figure there'll be plenty of time for me to travel the world when I get other stuff out of the way.'

'What other stuff?' she asked. 'Career stuff? Surely it's in your interests career-wise to have lived and worked overseas as so many of your colleagues do?'

Jake emptied the bucket and rinsed out the sponge at the tap. 'Is that why you're here?' he asked, glancing at her over his shoulder. 'To further your career?'

Her eyes moved out of range of his. 'Of course it is.'

He picked up the bucket of rinsing water. 'Three months isn't very long,' he said as he set to work on the car again.

'It's long enough.'

'To further your career or mend a broken heart?'

The air stiffened in silence.

'I haven't got a broken heart,' she said.

Jake looked at her over the top of the car. 'Looks like it to me.'

She straightened her slumped shoulders and sent him one of her Jane Austen looks. 'And I suppose you know all the signs because you've broken so many female hearts yourself,' she said.

'I haven't broken any just lately,' he said. 'Anyway, it's not something I set out to do deliberately.'

She gave a little laugh that was not even a distant cousin to humour. 'I'm sure you don't,' she said, kicking at one of the tyres with her foot. 'My ex claimed he didn't do it on purpose, either.'

'How long were you together?' Jake asked.

She let out a long sigh before she faced him. 'For ever.'

He came back around to her side and leaned against the car. 'Want to talk about it?'

Her eyes skittered away from his. 'Not particularly.'

'I take it he found someone else?' Jake said.

Her gaze was glazed with bitterness, like a coating of shellac. 'My best friend.'

'Ouch,' he said, wincing in empathy. 'That would've hurt.'

'It did.' She bit her lip until the blood drained away. 'It does…'

Jake hardly realised he had moved away from the car and put a hand on the top of her slim shoulder until he felt the lightning strike shock of the contact run up his arm from the cup of his palm.

Her eyes met his and locked.

Electricity zapped and fired.

Desire roared through his veins like a runaway freight train. He could see the answering flare in her grey gaze. He felt the gentle shudder of her flesh beneath his hand. He stood mesmerised as the tip of her tongue snaked out and brushed over her soft lips in a single heartbeat of time that seemed immeasurable.

He lowered his head fraction by fraction, frame by frame, like a film being played in slow motion. The stop signals and flashing red lights in the rational side of his brain were overruled by the need to taste the sweet pillow of her mouth, to press against those soft contours and forget about everything but the sensual energy that flowed in a spine-tingling current between them.

He cupped his other palm against the soft satiny curve of her cheek, watching as her serious smoky grey eyes registered the contact with a dilation of her pupils.

Her lips parted slightly, her vanilla-scented breath tantalising him as he came even closer.

The dark fan of her eyelashes lowered over her eyes, but just as he was about to make contact her eyes suddenly sprang open and she stumbled backwards out of his light hold.

'I'm sorry,' she said, blushing furiously. 'I can't do this.'

Jake gave a casual *whatever* shrug and put his hands out of temptation's way in the pockets of his shorts. 'No problem,' he said.

She pressed her lips together tightly for a moment, actively avoiding his gaze. 'I don't want you to get the wrong idea about me...'

'My bad,' Jake said. 'I overstepped the line. Blame my sister Rosie.'

She cautiously met his gaze. 'Your…sister?'

'I'm trying to win a bet,' he said. 'No sex this summer. I've just about made it too. Only twenty-two days to go.'

Her cheeks turned rosy red. 'How morally upright of you,' she said. 'So come the first of March anyone is pretty much fair game?'

He gave her a glinting look. 'I do have *some* standards.'

'Oh, yes,' she said with her customary hauteur. 'A strong working pulse. I almost forgot.'

Jake smiled wryly as he picked up his bucket. 'Do you want me to run a chamois over your car to dry it off?' he asked.

'No, thank you,' she said, with schoolmarmish primness.

He tapped the bonnet with his hand. 'Give me a shout if you need a jump start in the morning,' he said. 'I have the necessary equipment.'

'I'm quite sure I won't be needing *any* of your equipment,' she said, that dainty chin going up another notch.

'Well,' Jake said, giving her a deliberately smouldering look, 'you know where it is if and when you do.'

# CHAPTER SIX

KITTY was putting her things in the locker in the staff changing room the next morning when one of the nurses on duty came in.

'Hi, Dr Cargill,' the nurse said. 'I'm Cathy Oxley. I haven't been rostered on with you yet. How are you settling in?'

'Fine,' Kitty said. 'It's a bit of a steep learning curve. I'm still finding my feet.'

Cathy's brown eyes twinkled meaningfully. 'I'm sure our gorgeous boss is helping you with that after hours.'

Kitty felt her cheeks heat up. 'I'm not sure what you mean by that,' she said, closing her locker door with a little rattle. 'I'm not seeing Dr Chandler after hours.'

'Oh, sorry,' Cathy said. 'I must have got my wires crossed. I could've sworn someone said you two were dating. Mind you, it would be a first for him if you were.'

'A first?' Kitty frowned. 'In what way?'

'I don't think he's ever dated anyone on his immediate staff before,' Cathy said as she stored her bag in a locker two doors away from Kitty's. She closed and locked the locker and turned back to face Kitty. 'One of the nurses last year actually asked for a transfer to another department so he would take her out. Not that it lasted all that long. But that's Jake-break-your-heart-Chandler for you. It'll be a very special woman indeed who manages to lure him to an altar any time soon.'

Kitty turned and worked on smoothing over her tightly restrained hair in front of the mirror. 'Not all men are cut out for the responsibility of commitment and marriage,' she said. 'It's all a matter of maturity.'

'I don't think Jake would like to hear you describe him as immature,' Cathy said with a little chuckle.

'Men can be commitment-shy for all sorts of reasons, I guess. Particularly if they haven't had a great experience of commitment in their own family.'

'Jake doesn't talk about his background,' Cathy said. 'He's a bit of dark horse in that regard. I know he's got siblings. His brother's just as gorgeous in looks, apparently. A younger sister of one of the nurses on the neuro ward went out with him a couple of times.'

'Looks aren't everything,' Kitty said. 'What about character and values?'

'Our Jake's got those as well,' Cathy said. 'You just have to go searching for them. He doesn't wear his heart on his sleeve.'

'Has he even got a heart?' Kitty asked with an arch of one of her brows.

Cathy grinned as she shouldered open the locker room door. 'Last time I looked—but who knows? Maybe someone's stolen it by now.'

Kitty had barely been on the floor of the unit thirty seconds when Jake Chandler informed her there was a critical incident unfolding right outside the A&E department.

'Two teenagers have been knocked down by a

car,' he said, issuing orders to the nurses on duty as he strode through. 'Cathy, Tanya, get airway and trauma kits, hard collars, IV equipment and spinal boards.'

Kitty followed Jake and Lei and four nurses out to the street outside the A&E receiving area, where the police were diverting the traffic and securing the scene from bystanders.

She felt her heart pounding behind the framework of her ribs. She was used to dealing with patients in the unit, not out on the street. She had never attended a real accident, only mock-up ones.

Two kids—a girl and a boy—in their mid-teens were lying on the road. Horns were blaring. Sirens were screaming and lights were flashing. People were screaming and shouting. The police were doing their best to control the scene, but it was nothing short of mayhem given it was smack-bang in the middle of peak hour.

'Dr Cargill,' said Jake, calmly but with unmistakable authority. 'Take Cathy and Tanya and do a primary survey on the girl and tell me what equipment you need. Lei, take Lara and Tim and get started on the boy.'

Kitty started her assessment of the girl who was unconscious. 'AVPU is P,' she said. 'I don't have an airway.'

'Get the neck stable and get her intubated,' Jake ordered.

Kitty felt a flutter of panic rush through her stomach like a rapidly shuffled deck of cards. 'I can maintain her airway without intubating her out here.'

'You need to secure the airway and get the rest of the primary survey done now,' Jake said. 'We're not moving her until she's assessed. Do you want me to intubate her?'

'No,' Kitty said, mentally crossing her fingers and her toes. 'I can manage.'

'Good,' he said. 'Get it done and then give me the primary survey.' He turned to the registrar. 'Lei, what's your assessment?'

'GCS thirteen, Dr Chandler,' Lei said. 'Airway patent, multiple fractured right ribs and a flail segment. Probably right pneumothorax. Pulse one-twenty, BP one hundred on sixty. No external bleeding.'

Kitty kept working on her patient, wishing she were half as confident as the registrar appeared to be.

She tried to focus.

*To keep calm.*

This was not the time to doubt her skills. She had been trained for this. She had worked on similar cases inside A&E.

*Come on*, she gave herself a little pep talk. *You've intubated loads of patients before. Why should this one be any different?*

'Good work, Lei,' Jake was saying. 'Is it a tension pneumothorax?'

'No tension, Dr Chandler,' Lei said. 'Fair air entry and no mediastinal shift.'

'Brilliant,' Jake said. 'Get a collar on and do a quick secondary survey. Log roll and check the spine. If that's all, pack him up onto the spinal board, get in a cannula, get him inside and continue in there.'

'Will do.'

Kitty could feel the sweat pouring down between her shoulderblades as she tried again to intubate the girl. The sun was burning down like a blowtorch on the top of her scalp. Panic was no longer fluttering in the pit of her stomach; it was flapping like a bedsheet in a hurricane-force wind.

*This was not a dummy patient.*

This was someone's daughter, someone's little girl, someone's sister and someone's friend. If this young girl died someone's life—many people's lives—would be shattered.

The sun burned even more fiercely and the trickle of sweat down between the straps of her bra became a torrent. Her head started to pound as if a construction site had taken up residence inside. The sunlight was so bright her vision blurred. She blinked and white flashes floated past her eyes like silverfish.

'What's the problem?' Jake asked as he came over.

'This is not the ideal environment to do an intubation,' Kitty muttered in frustration. 'It's too bright and I can't see the cords.'

'Accidents don't happen in ideal environments,

Dr Cargill,' he said. 'We're not moving her until the airway and neck is secured. You stabilise her neck while I intubate.'

Kitty moved aside as Jake came around to the head of the patient and took over the laryngoscope. 'Hold the head from below,' he ordered.

She did as he directed and watched as he inserted the laryngoscope. It was genuinely a difficult task, which should have made Kitty feel less of a failure, but it was pretty obvious Jake had had extensive training and was far more experienced at resuscitating on site. Everything he did he did with cool and calm confidence. He kept his emotions in check. Not a muscle on his face showed any sign of personal distress or crisis. He was simply getting on with the job.

'Listen to the chest, Dr Cargill,' he said. 'What's the air entry?'

Kitty listened to the patient's chest. 'There's no air entry on the right and mediastinal shift to the left.'

'Get a needle in the chest,' he said. 'We can put a chest tube in inside.' He called out to the nurse. 'Kate—here. Ventilate the patient while I get the collar back on and get a drip in.'

Finally the patients were transferred inside and taken to ICU once stabilised.

'Good work, everyone,' Jake said, stripping off his gloves and tossing them in the bin.

Kitty couldn't help feeling she didn't deserve to be included in that statement. She concentrated on washing her hands at the basin, hanging her aching head down, feeling the sweat still sticky beneath her clothes.

'You too, Dr Cargill,' Jake said as he reached for some paper towels alongside her basin. 'That was a tough call.'

Kitty looked up at him. 'I was out of my depth and you know it,' she said.

'You'll get better once you do EMST,' he said. 'It's all a matter of confidence. The same skills apply inside here or outside there.'

'I was nearly roasted alive out there,' she said. 'It looked like you didn't even break a sweat.'

His dark blue gaze scanned her flushed face. 'You look like you caught the sun,' he said. 'Your nose is a little pink.'

'Great,' she said with a rueful grimace. 'More freckles.'

'Kisses from the sun,' he said. 'Or so my mother called them when I was a kid.'

'But you don't have any freckles.'

The corner of his mouth tipped up and a glint appeared in his eyes. 'None that you can see.'

Kitty flushed to the roots of her hair but stalwartly held his gaze. 'I'll pass on the guided tour, thanks very much,' she said.

'I wasn't offering one.'

His blue eyes played tug-of-war with hers in a moment that vibrated with palpable tension.

'Sorry to interrupt, Jake,' Gwen said as she approached. 'Your brother is here to see you. He's waiting in Reception. He told me to tell you it's important.'

Jake's expression tightened, and then locked down to a blank impenetrable mask. 'Call me on my mobile if anything urgent comes in,' he said gruffly to Kitty. 'I'll be ten minutes.'

Gwen let out a sigh as Jake disappeared through the entrance to A&E. 'I wish Jake would tell me what's going on.'

Kitty frowned. 'Going on?'

'With Robbie,' Gwen said. 'I can tell Jake's worried sick about him but he won't talk about it. I guess he's used to dealing with his family on his own. God knows he's been doing it long enough.'

'What do you mean?' Kitty asked.

'Jake's mother was killed in a car accident when he was sixteen,' Gwen said. 'And that's another thing he won't talk about. I only heard about it because one of the paramedics who attended the accident worked with my husband in the fire department. A drunk driver hit Jake's mother head-on. She made it to hospital but died a few hours later.'

'That's terrible,' Kitty said. 'What about his father?'

Gwen rolled her eyes. 'That's another one of Jake's no-go areas,' she said. 'I don't think he's seen his father since he was a kid. I don't think Robbie has even met him.'

'Who looked after Jake and his siblings after their mother was killed?' Kitty asked.

'I think they stayed with his mother's parents

for a bit, but it didn't last,' Gwen said. 'They'd disowned their daughter when she hooked up with Jake's father. They didn't even know the kids when they were plonked on their doorstep. Jake got his own place as soon as he could afford it and made his own way. Can't have been easy. He's done such a good job of taking care of them all, but now Robbie's got some sort of issue. God knows what it is. Jake certainly won't let on.'

Kitty looked towards the doors Jake had just gone through. She thought back to her conversation with him about why he hadn't travelled abroad. Had he stayed home in order to watch over his siblings? How had he coped financially? Had his mother left them well provided for or did he have to struggle to make ends meet? What else had he sacrificed to be there for his family?

The image of him as a protective father figure was at odds with her impression of him as a fun-loving, laid-back playboy. But then she thought of the day she'd seen him at the beach with his young nephew. No one could ask for a more devoted uncle and mentor. Strict but fair, strong but nurturing—all the things young kids and in particular boys needed to grow. Jake had apparently had no such mentor himself. Instead he had been the man of the house for most of his thirty-four years.

Kitty turned and saw Gwen looking at her speculatively. 'What were you two talking about just then, anyway?' Gwen asked. 'You looked rather cosy.'

Kitty felt a flush pass over her cheeks. 'It was just...nothing.'

Gwen gave her a motherly smile of caution. 'Tread carefully, my dear,' she said. 'He's a gorgeous man in looks and in temperament, but he doesn't play for keeps.'

'I don't know how many times I have to tell everyone I'm not interested in Jake Chandler,' Kitty said with an irritated frown.

Gwen's look was long and measuring. 'Not that you wouldn't make a lovely couple or anything,' she said. 'I can see the sparks that fly between you.'

'I'm sure you're imagining it,' Kitty said, still frowning. 'Personally, I think he can't wait until

I hop on that plane back to Britain. He thinks I'm not up to the task.'

'You're handling things just fine,' Gwen said. 'Jake's not one to stroke egos unnecessarily. If he was unhappy with your work he'd soon let you know.'

Kitty gave her a grim look. 'That's exactly what I'm afraid of,' she said, and turned back to the unit.

# CHAPTER SEVEN

KITTY didn't see Jake face-to-face for the rest of her shift. He had come back to the unit after a few minutes, but she had been tied up with a patient with chronic asthma whose condition hadn't been properly managed by either the patient or his doctor. By the time she'd sorted the middle-aged man out Jake had been busy with other patients.

But when she was walking along the Bondi shopping and café strip later that evening, in search of somewhere to grab some dinner, she saw him coming towards her.

He looked preoccupied. There was a frown between his brows and his jaw looked as if it had been carved from stone. He didn't even see her until she was practically under his nose.

'Dr Chandler?'

Her softly spoken greeting didn't even register,

so she reached out and touched him on the bare tanned skin of his forearm with her fingertips.

'Jake?'

He jumped as if she had probed him with an electrode. 'Oh,' he said, absently rubbing at his arm. 'It's you.'

'Yes...' Kitty shifted her weight from foot to foot. 'Are you OK?'

His marble mask stayed in place. 'Sure. Why wouldn't I be?'

'I just thought you might like to...talk.'

Something moved across his gaze, leaving in its wake a layer of ice. 'About what?'

'Gwen told me you were having some trouble with your brother and I thought—'

'You thought what, Dr Cargill?' he asked with a mocking look. 'That you'd offer your sweet little shoulder for me to cry on?'

Kitty held his glacial gaze for a beat or two before giving up. 'I've obviously caught you at a bad time,' she said, stepping away from him. 'I'm sorry, I didn't mean to interfere.'

She had walked past three shopfronts before he caught up with her. He didn't touch her. He walked alongside her, shoulder to shoulder—well, not exactly shoulder to shoulder, given he was so much taller. Kitty was wearing ballet flats, which put the top of her head in line with the top of his shoulder. She felt the warmth of his body. She had to fight to keep walking in a straight line in case her body betrayed her with its traitorous, shameless desires.

'Don't let me keep you,' she said, sending him a sideways glance that made her loose hair momentarily brush against his arm. She grabbed at the wayward strands and fixed them firmly behind her ear.

'Sorry,' he said in a gruff tone. 'That was uncalled-for.'

'It's OK,' she said, only marginally mollified.

They walked a few more paces in silence. Kitty wasn't sure what to say, so said nothing. She figured if he wanted to talk to her he would. Every time she sneaked a glance at him he was frowning broodingly. His shoulders looked tight and were hunched forward slightly, as if he was carrying an invisible weight that was incredibly burdensome.

'Have you got any siblings?' he finally asked.

'No, there's just me,' Kitty said.

'Happy childhood?'

'Mostly.'

'Are your parents still married to each other?' he asked.

Kitty gave him another sideways glance, trying to ignore the way her heart kicked in her chest when she encountered the unfathomable darkness of his sapphire-blue gaze. 'My parents didn't get married in the first place,' she said. 'They met at a free love commune. They're still together, more or less. They occasionally have other partners. They have what they call an "open" relationship.'

His eyebrows lifted. 'I wouldn't have picked you as a hippy couple's kid,' he said. 'Did the stork get the wrong address or something?'

Kitty couldn't hold back a little rueful smile. 'My parents have spent a great deal of the last twenty-six years looking at each other in a kind of dumbfounded way,' she said. 'They were hoping for a free-spirited indie child much like themselves. I constantly embarrass them.'

His mouth kicked up at the corners. 'I just bet you do.'

Kitty caught a whiff of his cologne as he raised a hand to brush his hair back off his forehead. The faint hint of hard-working male was like a potent elixir to her nostrils. She even felt herself leaning closer to catch more of his alluring scent.

He met her gaze again, holding it with the dark intensity of his. 'I lost my mother when I was sixteen,' he said. 'And my father...' He paused, a frown cutting his forehead in two, and the lines and planes of his face clouding. 'My father left us before my brother was born. My two sisters can barely remember him. None of us have seen or heard of him since he left. Not even when Mum died.'

'I'm very sorry,' Kitty said. 'Life can be pretty brutal at times. You must have had a hard time of it.'

'Yeah, you could say that,' he said, stepping aside for a group of teenagers carrying body-boards to pass between them.

'What about your sisters?' Kitty asked when

he didn't offer anything else once they had resumed walking side by side. 'What do they do?'

'Jen's a hairdresser,' he said. 'She's saving up to buy her own salon. Rosie works part-time as a teacher's aide. She's studying to be a teacher.'

A small silence passed.

'And your brother?' Kitty asked.

His gaze cut to hers. 'Didn't Gwen tell you during your little heart-to-heart session? I'm sure she along with everyone else at the hospital has a theory or two on why Robbie's running amok.'

'I didn't probe her for information,' she said. 'She didn't know much in any case. She simply told me she sensed that your brother seemed to have some…issues.'

'Issues.' He gave a harsh laugh. 'That's how everyone makes excuses for any sort of bad behaviour today. They've got *issues*. Do you know what bugs me about that? It's *always* someone else's fault. It's a get out of jail free card. No one has to take responsibility for their own actions any more. There's always someone else to blame. Bad childhood or bad parenting. Or in my case practically no parenting. I hate that victim mentality that everyone adopts these days. It achieves nothing. You just have to get on with life. There's no point wishing things were different. You get what you get and you damn well have to deal with it.'

Kitty walked with him for a few more paces. 'I guess different people cope with things in different ways,' she said after a moment. 'What makes one person stronger makes another one crumble.'

'Yeah, well, I just wish my brother would snap out of this phase of his,' he said. 'I'm sick and tired of cleaning up his mess.'

'You sound just like a concerned parent,' she said. 'At least you'll have had plenty of practice when it comes to having your own kids.'

His expression became even more dark and brooding. 'No way,' he said. 'I'm not making that mistake.'

'You don't want kids?'

'Why would I want kids when I've already brought up three?' he asked.

'Helping to rear your siblings is not the same as having your own children,' Kitty said.

He gave a grunt. 'It is for me,' he said. 'I've

made enough packed lunches to last me a life-time.'

'Having children is much more than just packed lunches,' she said.

'Yeah,' he said. 'And don't I know it. The cute chubby cheeks stage is over before you know it. Then it's suddenly all about spending hours awake at night wondering where they are and who they're with and what they're doing. I'm not putting myself through that again. No way.'

'What about marriage?' she asked. 'Are you against that too?'

'I'm not against it in principle,' he said. 'I have plenty of friends who are married and it seems to work for them. I just don't think I'm cut out for it. I think I'd get bored with the same person.'

'Maybe you haven't met the right person yet.'

He shrugged indifferently. 'Maybe.'

They'd walked halfway along the next block when Jake suddenly stopped and turned to look at her. 'Have you had dinner?' he asked.

'No, I was just about to get some when I saw you.'

'Have dinner with me.'

She arched a brow at him. 'Are you asking or telling me?'

'Are you refusing or accepting?'

'I'm thinking about it.'

'What's to think about?' he asked. 'You're hungry and you need food.'

'It's not that simple...'

'Are you worried about the boyfriend back home in Britain?'

Kitty avoided his penetrating gaze. 'It has nothing to do with Charles,' she said. 'I don't want people to talk.'

'They're already talking,' he said. 'Besides, what's one casual dinner going to do?' He stopped outside a bar and grill restaurant. 'Is this OK? A friend of mine owns it. He'll squeeze us in without a booking.'

Kitty met his impossibly blue gaze with her guarded one. 'So it's not a date or anything?' she asked.

'No,' he said, giving her a glinting smile. 'I'd have to pay my sister a thousand bucks if so.'

Kitty tried not to blush but with little success.

'So an official date with you usually leads to sex, does it?'

He held the door of the restaurant open for her. 'It depends.'

'On what?'

'Chemistry. Animal attraction. Lust.'

Kitty pursed her lips disapprovingly even though her skin tingled and prickled as his gaze held hers. 'What about getting to know someone as a person first?' she asked. 'Finding common ground, similar values and interests, mutual admiration and respect?'

His gaze moved from her eyes to her mouth. Something shifted in the pit of her belly as his eyes meshed with hers once more. Their dark glittering intensity triggered a primal response she had no control over. Fluttery fairy-soft footsteps of excitement danced along the floor of her stomach at the thought of him pressing that sinfully sensual mouth against hers, having his arms go around her and crush her to his hard tall frame, feeling his arousal potent and persistent against the yielding softness of her body. She drew in a little shuddering breath, wondering if he could sense how deeply affected she was by him.

*But of course*, she thought.

He was a practised flirt. A charmer—a playboy who loved nothing better than indulging the flesh without the restraints of a formal relationship—a born seducer who loved and left his partners without a second thought.

Falling in love with him would be the biggest mistake of her life. She knew it and yet there was something about him that drew her inexorably to him. She felt the magnetic force of him even now. The way his gaze tethered her to him, those ocean-blue depths communicating without words the desire that crackled like an electrical current between them.

'I find out just about all I need to know about the other person with the first kiss,' he said.

'Oh, really?'

'You'd be surprised how much information that reveals.'

Kitty gave him an arch look. 'You mean other than the flavour of their toothpaste?'

He smiled that glinting smile. 'Having dinner

with them is another revelation,' he said. 'Picky eaters tend to have body issues. A healthy appetite is a good sign, but someone who is keen to try different cuisines or exotic flavours gets my attention every time.'

Kitty felt heat rise up from the soles of her feet to her face. What would he think of her cardboard meals of late? 'You seem to have it down to a science,' she said.

'Hey, Jake!' A stocky blond-haired man came over with a twinkling smile on his face. 'A cosy, romantic table for two?'

Kitty gave Jake a look. 'How many times have you been here?'

'Lost count,' Jake said, and grinned at his mate. 'How're you doing, Brad? Hot in the kitchen?'

'That's why I'm out here,' Brad said, and smiling at Kitty added, 'So this is...?'

'Dr Kitty Cargill,' Jake said.

Brad's eyebrows lifted. 'Bringing work home with you, Jake?'

'It's not what you think,' Jake said.

'Sure,' Brad said with a grin. 'Follow me. I have just the table for you.'

Once Brad had left them settled with drinks, Kitty met Jake's gaze across the small intimate table that was positioned in the quietest part of the restaurant. 'Let me guess,' she said. 'At about ten p.m. or so a woman will come past the table selling roses.'

He gave her a slanting smile. 'Do you want one?'

'Certainly not!'

He reached over to top up her water glass from the frosted bottle on the table. 'So, tell me about Charles.'

Kitty watched as the bubbles from the mineral water rose in a series of vertical lines like tiny necklaces to the surface of her glass. 'There's not much to tell,' she said. 'We grew up together. I can't think of a time in my life when Charles hasn't been a part of it. We did everything together. I thought we'd continue to do everything together.' She released a little sigh and met Jake's gaze. 'I was so busy planning our future that I didn't notice what was going on in the present.'

'Do you still love him?'

Kitty looked at the bubbles again, her finger

tracing the dew on the outside of the glass. 'I think there's a part of me that will always love Charles,' she said. 'I loved his family too. I liked that they were so...so normal. I felt at home with them. I blended in as if I had always been there.'

She looked up to find his dark blue gaze centred on hers. He had a way of looking at her that made her whole body break out in a shiver. She became aware of every cell of her skin, from the top of her tingling scalp, right to the very soles of her feet.

She gave herself a mental shake and reached for her wine glass. 'What did your brother want when he came to the unit today?' she asked.

A mask slipped over his features. 'I thought we were talking about you,' he said.

'We were,' she said. 'But now it's your turn to talk about you.'

'What if I don't want to talk about me?'

'Then talk about your brother.'

He frowned as he reached for his own wine glass, but he didn't drink from it. He just sat there twirling the stem round and round between his finger and thumb. 'I hate talking about my

brother,' he said. 'Talking doesn't change anything. He's a fully-grown adult and yet just lately
he's been acting like a kid. He used to have a
part-time job to fund his way through university, but he lost that over some run-in with the
boss. He's been putting the hard word on Rosie
and Jen for money and when he's really getting
desperate he comes to me.'

'Where does he live?'

'In some doss house in the inner city,' he said,
scraping a hand through his hair. He made a de-
spairing sound. 'My kid brother bunks down
with every other desperado on the streets. My
mother is probably spinning in her grave.'

Kitty put out a hand and touched his arm. His
muscles flexed then stilled under her touch.

After a long moment his eyes met hers. 'Do
you know what gets me?' he asked. 'He had
everything going so well. He was a straight A
student. He was up for a university prize in engineering. He's so damn bright—much brighter
than me. I've had to work damn hard to get
where I've got. But he's thrown it all away. It's
such a damn waste.'

'Is he doing drugs?' Kitty asked.

He rubbed a hand over his face. 'I don't know if he's touched the hard stuff. He says not, but how can I trust him? He probably doesn't remember from one day to the next what he's been doing.'

'What about rehab?' she asked.

His eyes hit hers. 'You think I haven't tried that?' he asked. 'I even paid up-front for a private clinic, but he didn't show up on admission day. I couldn't find him for a fortnight. The clinic had a waiting list a mile long so I couldn't get him in even when I found him.'

'Sometimes it's hard for family members to be the ones to help,' Kitty said. 'You're too close and they don't always want to listen.'

His fingers tightened around the stem of his glass. 'The sick irony is I've spent the last twenty-four years of my life being a substitute father for my sisters and brother,' he said. 'Don't get me wrong—I was glad to be able to do something. My mother wanted each of us to have better opportunities than she'd had. It was up to me to see that her vision for us as a family was fulfilled.'

'That's why you've never travelled, isn't it?' Kitty asked.

'I had a ticket booked once.' He gave her a brief glance before focussing on the contents of his glass. 'I had all my siblings sorted, or so I thought. I was going to head off to Europe for a couple of months. Kick my heels up a bit, have a life, have some fun without the pressure of re-sponsibility.'

'What happened?'

He looked at her again, the line of his mouth grim. 'Rosie came to me late one night and told me she was pregnant. She'd known for weeks but had been too scared to tell me. She was just nineteen years old. Still a kid herself. I couldn't leave her to deal with that, even for a couple of months. I didn't want her to feel pressured into a termination. I wanted her to feel supported in whatever she decided to do. Her boyfriend was useless. And what sort of brother would I be if I just flew out of the country at a time like that?'

'From what I can tell you've been an amazing brother and uncle,' Kitty said. 'Look at the way you gave that party for her. And then you took your nephew surfing, on top of a full day at work.'

'It's not enough,' he said. 'I can't be there all the time.'

'I'm sure no one expects you to,' she said. 'You're entitled to your own life.'

His eyes came back to hers, a wry smile kicking up the corners of his mouth. 'That's one very soft shoulder you've got there, Dr Cargill,' he said.

Kitty smiled back. 'Glad to be of service.'

It was close to eleven when Jake walked Kitty to the door of her town house. A light sea breeze had come in and taken the stifling heat out of the evening, bringing with it the tang of brine from the ocean.

She stood fumbling with her keys in the lock, conscious of him standing behind her, his tall frame within touching distance of hers. She could smell the hint of lemon in his aftershave. She could even hear his breathing—steady and slow, unlike hers, which was skittering all over the place.

'Do you want me to unlock it for you?' he asked.

'No, I'm fine… Oh, damn,' she said as she dropped her keys with a loud clatter to the tiled floor.

He bent down, scooped them off the floor and handed them to her. His fingers brushed against her open palm, sending electric shocks right up her arm. 'You don't need to be nervous, Dr Cargill,' he said.

'Nervous?' Kitty tucked a strand of hair behind her ear, her tongue sneaking out quickly to moisten her mouth. 'Why on earth would I be nervous?'

He smiled at her. It was the tiniest movement of his lips and yet it unravelled her insides like a skein of wool thrown by a spin-bowler. 'When was the last time you asked a man in for coffee?' he asked.

She tore her gaze away from his sexily slanted mouth. 'When I was in junior high,' she said. 'But it wasn't for coffee. It was for orange juice.'

'Cute.'

Kitty unlocked the door and then faced him. 'I have coffee if you'd like some,' she said, waving a hand in the vague direction of the kitchen.

His sapphire gaze glinted. 'Got any orange juice?'

'Fresh or reconstituted?'

'You can't beat fresh,' he said as he closed the door behind him with a soft click. 'It tastes completely different.'

'I can never tell the difference,' she said, with a huskiness that was nothing like her usual dulcet tones. 'But then, I guess I'm not much of an orange juice connoisseur.'

The space in the foyer seemed to shrink now that he shared it with her. The air seemed to tighten, to crackle and vibrate with an energy that made the hairs on her head push away from her scalp. The skin on her arms went up in goosebumps and her stomach pitched and tilted as he closed the distance between them with a single step.

His hooded gaze zeroed in on her mouth as he planted a hand on the wall beside her head.

'This is the part where you're supposed to ask me what the hell I think I'm doing,' he said in a gravel-rough tone.

'I am?'

'Yeah,' he said. 'But since you missed your cue maybe we can jump ahead to the next bit.'

Kitty's heart flapped like a shredded truck tyre on tarmac. 'What's the next bit?' she asked in a soft whisper.

His warm minty breath caressed her parted lips as he inched closer and closer. 'Why don't I show you?' he said, and then he sealed her mouth with his.

# CHAPTER EIGHT

KITTY felt a shockwave ripple through her body when his lips made that first contact with hers. His lips moved against hers in a slow, sensual manner, tasting, teasing and tempting her into a heated response that made the base of her spine melt like butter and every hair on her head tremble with delight. His kiss was soft and experimental, a tantalising assault on her senses that made her skin tauten all over in fiery response.

He threaded his hands through her hair, his fingers splaying over her tingling scalp as he scorched the seam of her mouth with the bold stroke of his tongue.

She opened to him and the world exploded in a burst of colour and leaping flares of searing heat. His tongue tangled with hers in a sexy dance that made her heart race and her belly flip and then flop.

This was no tame boy-next-door kiss. This was a man's kiss—the kiss of a full-blooded man who wanted sex and wanted it *now*.

Kitty felt the ridge of hard male desire against her quivering belly. She felt the instinctual, primal tug of her flesh towards it. She shifted her body against his, her heart skipping a beat when she heard the deep sound of male approval come from his throat.

Her breasts were jammed up against the hard plane of his chest. She had never been so aware of them before. They swelled and strained behind the lace cage of her bra, hungry for more intimate contact.

She shivered when his hands went to her hips, holding her closer to the cradle of his pelvis. Every delicious male inch of him was imprinted on her flesh. She felt the pounding roar of his blood through his clothes. It echoed the rampant need that was surging inside her.

His mouth continued its fiery exchange with hers, his tongue calling hers into a brazen tango that mimicked the need charging through his body as well as her own.

He shifted one of his hands from her hips to the small of her back, the subtle pressure sending her senses into a crazy spin. Desire licked along her flesh like a trail of racing flames, her need as insistent as a tribal drumbeat deep inside her body.

His hand on her hip moved upwards in a slow-moving caress that stopped just below her right breast. She felt her nerves tighten in awareness. The tingling and twitching of her flesh was almost unbearable. She pressed herself against him in a silent signal of female want, a desperate plea for him to satisfy the deepest yearnings of her body.

Kitty kissed him back with brazen hunger. Her lips nibbled and nipped at his. Her tongue swirled and circled and swept against his in a sensual combat that made her spine turn to liquid. He fought back with another deep groan of approval and pulled her even closer to the rampant need of his body.

She fisted a hand in his shirt and he plunged deeper into her mouth, his strongly muscled thighs moving against hers to nudge her back against the wall. The body-to-body contact fuelled her desire to an unmanageable level. She pushed herself up on tiptoe so she could feel more of his hard heat against her feminine need. Her insides melted and pulsed with longing. Desire was like a runaway train. It was flashing past every station, siding or level crossing of caution and common sense she had erected in her brain.

Jake lifted his mouth off hers and looked down at her, his expression darkly satirical. 'Well, I guess that clears up that little detail,' he said.

Kitty blinked herself out of her sensual daze and stepped out of his hold. She tucked a strand of hair behind her ear, feeling gauche and flustered. 'I'm not sure what you mean,' she said.

His mouth kicked up in a wry smile. 'You're not the shy, uptight type after all, are you?'

Kitty pressed her lips together for a moment. 'I'm sure I don't need to tell you you're a very good kisser.'

'You pack a pretty awesome punch yourself, Dr Cargill,' he said.

She tried to act casual about it, affecting a pose

of indifference that belied the turmoil she felt inside. 'Do you still want coffee?'

He reached out and passed one of his bent knuckles over the curve of her cheek in a light caress, his eyes so dark she couldn't tell where his pupils began and ended. 'You don't really think I came in here for coffee, do you?' he asked.

Kitty swept the tip of her tongue over her kiss-swollen lips, her heart skipping all over the place. 'I guess not...'

He held her gaze captive for a long heart-stopping moment. 'I want you.'

The blunt statement shocked and yet thrilled her. Charles had waited *years* before asking her to sleep with him. 'But for how long?' she asked.

'That's not a question anyone can answer specifically,' he said. 'Relationships run their course. Some last days, others weeks, others years.'

She toyed with a button on his shirt rather than meet his gaze. 'Yours don't last years, though, do they?' she said.

It seemed a long time before he answered. 'I'm

not promising anything long-term, Kitty. You're only here until the end of April. It wouldn't be fair to pretend this could turn into an affair of a lifetime.'

Kitty raised her eyes to his. 'Because you don't want to fall in love.'

'You don't have to be in love with someone to have great sex,' he said. 'Aren't your parents proof of that?'

Her shoulders went down on a little sigh as she moved away. 'I'm not like my parents,' she said. 'I couldn't bear to live the way they do. I don't want to play musical beds with faceless strangers. I want security. I want love. I want marriage and babies and happy ever after.'

He gave a cynical crack of laughter. 'You want a fairytale that doesn't exist in the real world. Fifty percent of marriages end up in divorce. The other fifty live snappily ever after.'

She threw him an exasperated look. 'There's no point arguing with you. I can see you've collated enough evidence to support your cynical take on things. But there are plenty of relationships that last the distance. I see them all the time in A&E. Old couples who've spent a whole lifetime loving each other. I *want* that. I want to be with someone for my whole life—not a month here or there or a measly week or two.'

'Then I'm not your man,' he said, his expression stony, his voice even harder. 'I'm happy to have a bit of fun, but don't expect anything else from me.'

Kitty held that steely blue gaze. 'I feel sorry for men like you, Jake. You have plenty of fun now, but what about later? What about when you're old and sick and no one wants you any more?'

A muscle flexed in his jaw. 'I'll take my chances.'

'You'll end up lonely and alone,' she said. 'You'll have no shared memories of the phases of life you've journeyed through. No children to share your genes. No grandchild—'

'Look,' he said, cutting her short. 'I get what you're saying. Do you think I haven't thought through all of that? Of course I have. I just can't make promises I'm not sure I'll be able to keep.'

Kitty nailed him with a flinty look. 'You don't *want* to make promises.'

He held her gaze for a second or two before he blew out a breath on a long exhale. He tipped up her chin using two fingers, while his thumb moved back and forth over the cushion of her bottom lip. 'It wouldn't work, you know,' he said. 'You. Me. Us. You're too innocent for someone as hard-boiled as me. I'd end up walking all over you.'

'I know how to take care of myself.'

'Do you, Kitty?' he asked looking at her intently. 'Do you really?'

Her heart tripped as his gaze centred on her mouth. Heat pooled in her belly and her legs felt that betraying tremble again. 'Of course I do,' she said. 'I'm a big girl now.'

He brushed an imaginary hair away from her face. 'Even big girls can get their hearts broken.'

'So can big boys.'

He gave her a twisted smile as he reached for the door. 'Not this big boy.'

'You're not truly alive if you don't allow yourself to be open to happiness and to hurt,' she said. 'It's what makes life so rich and rewarding—the highs and the lows and all the bits in between.'

'Goodnight, Dr Cargill,' he said. 'Sweet dreams.'

Kitty blew out a breath when the door clicked shut behind him. 'Watch it, my girl,' she said in an undertone. 'Just watch it, OK?'

'Where's Kitty?' Gwen asked, looking past Jake's shoulders when he arrived at the new staff welcome drinks on Friday night. 'I thought she might be coming with you.'

Jake took one of the light beers off a tray that was being handed around by one of the interns. 'Then you thought wrong,' he said.

Gwen angled her head at him. 'What's going on with you two?'

'Nothing.' He took a sip of froth off the top of his beer.

'You had dinner with her,' Gwen said. 'Brad told me when I had lunch with my daughter at the grill yesterday.'

He shrugged. 'So?'

'Don't break her heart, Jake.'

'I have no intention of doing any such thing.'

'She's not your type.'

Jake frowned as he put his beer on the chest-high drinks stand beside him. 'That's surely up to her to decide, isn't it?'

Gwen lifted her brows. 'I'm just saying.'

'Then don't,' he said, shooting her a look.

'How is Robbie?'

He shifted his gaze, his left hand tightening to a fist inside his trouser pocket. 'I'd rather not talk about my brother right now.'

'You never want to talk about him, Jake,' Gwen said. 'You used to chat about him all the time. How well he was doing. How nice it was to have him drop by with his friends. What's going on? Is he in some sort of trouble?'

Jake glared at her. 'Leave it, Gwen, OK? I don't want everyone talking about what a crap job I've done of watching out for my brother. He's an adult. I can't control him any more.'

'No one could possibly criticise you for what you've done for your family, Jake,' she said gently.

He let out a weary breath. 'Sorry, Gwen,' he said. 'I know you mean well. It's just that things are pretty tough right now. Robbie's being so irresponsible. I don't know how to handle him any more. It's like I'm dealing with someone else entirely.'

'Jim and I had a rough trot with one of our boys a few years back,' Gwen said. 'Matt gave us a couple of years of hell but he eventually grew out of it. Maybe Robbie's just going through a similar thing.'

Jake looked at her. 'When he first started acting up I thought he was sick or something,' he said. 'It was so out of character for him to be partying hard and neglecting his studies.'

'Did he see a doctor?'

'Yeah,' he said. 'I sent him to his GP for a battery of tests.'

'All clear?'

'Apparently,' he said. 'He didn't show me the scans. He said the GP told him there was nothing wrong. It was a long shot in any case. I've met stacks of parents of wayward kids who've insisted there must be something clinically wrong. It's the first thing you think of. No one wants to think their kid or brother or sister wilfully chooses to go and stuff up their life.'

'It's a stage a lot of young people seem to go through these days,' Gwen said. 'They like to kick up their heels before they settle down. Robbie's a good lad. You've always done the right thing by him. Hopefully he'll sort himself out before too much longer.'

'Yeah,' Jake said on another sigh. 'That what I'm hoping.'

'Aren't you supposed to be at the drinks thing tonight?' Cathy Oxley asked in A&E.

Kitty leafed through the blood results she had been waiting for. 'Yes, but I got held up with a patient.'

'All work and no play,' Cathy said in a singsong voice.

Kitty's gaze narrowed in concentration as she looked at the white cell count in front of her.

'Is something wrong?' Cathy asked.

Kitty lowered the sheaf of papers. 'Lara Fletcher,' she said. 'The twenty-four-year-old in Bay Four with breathlessness and swollen ankles. She's been back and forth to her GP for months with a host of vague symptoms. Not once has he or anyone else ordered a blood test. She's been fobbed off by two other medical clinics. One of them even gave her antidepressants, telling her she was depressed.'

'You found something?' Cathy asked, looking over her shoulder.

'Aplastic anaemia,' Kitty said heavily. 'How could that have been missed for all this time?'

'Not everyone is as meticulous as you.'

'All it took was a blood test.'

'Tell that to Jake Chandler next time he bawls you out for over-testing the patients,' Cathy said with a little wink.

'I will,' Kitty said.


'I didn't realise you were working this weekend,' said Trish Wellington, one of the more senior A&E specialists, when Jake came on duty on Saturday evening.

'I'm just doing a fill-in shift for David Godfrey,' Jake said. 'He's going to his sister's wedding.'

'Well, how about that?' Trish said with a speculative smile. 'Kitty Cargill's doing a double tonight. Mike called in sick at the last minute.'

Jake slung his stethoscope around his neck. 'I hope she's not overdoing it,' he said.

Trish leaned against the wall as she toyed with her hospital lanyard. 'She's a sharp little tack, isn't she?'

Jake soaped up his hands at the basin. 'She's competent enough.'

'Pretty little thing,' Trish said. 'Gorgeous grey eyes.'

'Haven't noticed.'

Trish laughed as she pushed herself away from the wall. '*So* glad I've worked here long enough to see it.'

He frowned at her darkly. 'Long enough to see what?' he asked.

She pointed at his chest. 'To see your heart get a run for its money,' she said.

Jake rolled his eyes. 'Oh, for pity's sake.'

'Dr Chandler?'

Jake felt the hairs on his arms lift up when that posh little voice sounded behind him. He turned and looked at Kitty's heart-shaped face looking up at him. She had smudges under her grey eyes and her skin was paler than usual, making the light sprinkling of freckles on her nose stand out.

'Dr Cargill,' he said formally. 'Thanks for doing overtime.'

'That's OK,' she said.

A beat of silence ticked past.

'Was there something else?' he asked.

'I'm sorry I didn't make it to the drinks thing,' she said. 'I hope you didn't think I snubbed... everyone?'

'I was only there for a couple of minutes my-self.'

'Oh...' Her expression faltered for a moment. 'Well, I got held up with a patient.'

'Taking down their family tree, were we?' he asked.

Her eyes blinked and then hardened like frost. 'No,' she said. 'I diagnosed a blood disorder that had gone undetected for several months. I lost count of how many GPs the patient had seen. Not one of them performed a blood screen on her.'

'It happens.'

She frowned at him. 'How can it happen? How can someone slip through the cracks like that?'

'GPs are pushed for time just like everyone else in the medical profession,' Jake said. 'The larger medical clinics are problematic because the patient doesn't always see the same doctor each visit. There's not much continuity.'

'Then all the more reason to check and double-check,' she said.

'Testing every patient for every disease is expensive and time-wasting,' he said. 'Diagnostic skills vary between doctors, but mostly they get it right.'

'Not in this case,' she said. 'That young woman's outcome could be severely compromised.'

'We can't save everyone, Dr Cargill,' he said. 'There will always be people who slip through the system.'

'I don't want to miss *anyone*,' she said. 'It's our job to diagnose and treat patients, not fob them off with a couple of painkillers.'

'You can't CT scan every patient who comes through the door,' Jake argued. 'Not on this campus, in any case.'

Her grey eyes challenged his. 'Are you forbidding me from conducting the tests I deem appropriate?' she asked.

'I would hope your diagnostic skills are of a standard such that you don't require exposing a patient to high levels of radiation in order to confirm your diagnosis.'

'I'd rather not leave patients' lives up to gut feeling,' she said with an insolent look.

'What do you mean by that?' he asked.

Her grey eyes flashed at him. 'You can't possibly get it right all of the time,' she said. 'It's not a matter of guesswork or intuition. We have to rely on cold, hard science.'

'The human body isn't an exact science,' he said. 'Patients don't always give a complete history. Tests can be inconclusive. We need to be able to understand anatomy and physiology in order make a correct diagnosis.'

'Will that be all, Dr Chandler?' she asked stiffly.

Jake looked at her mouth and felt a tidal
wave of raw, primal need course through him.
He couldn't stop thinking about that kiss. He
thought of how soft her mouth was, how sweet it
had tasted, how yielding it had been, how tentative and shy her tongue had been and then how
brazen and uncontrollable it had become when
she had let herself go. He thought of how her
slim little body had pressed against his as if she
had been tailored exactly to his specifications.
He thought of how much he wanted to kiss her
again, to move his hands over her creamy skin
without the barrier of clothes. He wanted to run
his hands through the chestnut silk of her hair,
to breathe in its flowery fragrance.

*He wanted her.*

Had he ever wanted someone more? It was this
wretched bet, that was what it was. It had to be.
He'd been celibate too long. He wasn't cut out for
the life of a monk. It wasn't that he was developing an attachment to Kitty. She wasn't staying
in Australia long enough to consider anything
more than a casual fling. She would probably go
back when her term was over and pick up again

with someone from her side of the tracks—not someone with dependent siblings, not to mention the debt and drama that came along for the ride.

If she hooked up with him it would be a package deal. How long before she would get sick of sharing him with his siblings and nephew? His career was demanding enough. Having to spread himself so thinly didn't make for ideal relationship-building conditions. He wasn't emotionally available. He didn't want to be. He didn't want to need someone so much he couldn't function without them. He had seen it first-hand. His mother had been absolutely devastated by the desertion of his father. Jake had lain awake at night listening to her sob her heart out in the bedroom next door. It had taken her years to recover, and even then there had been a part of her that had never fully returned. She had gone from a vibrant and fully engaged mother to a person who trudged through life with resolution rather than joy.

Jake brought his gaze to Kitty's defiant one. 'That will be all, Dr Cargill,' he said. 'For now.'

# CHAPTER NINE

'SO HOW'S it going with your gorgeous boss?' Julie asked when she phoned Kitty a couple of days later.

'Next question.'

Julie laughed. 'That bad, huh?'

Kitty paced the kitchen of her town house. 'He's the most maddening man I've ever met,' she said. 'I thought I was getting to know him a little bit. He's really nice when he's not playing the big bad boss. He was really supportive when we had this crazy emergency outside the hospital the other day. And he even told me about his family circumstances over dinner, and—'

'Dinner?' Julie said. 'Hey, back up a bit. You didn't tell me you had dinner with him. When was that?'

'It wasn't a date or anything,' Kitty said. 'We ran into each other and it sort of…happened.'

'What sort of happened?'

Kitty closed her mind to that kiss. 'Nothing happened,' she said. 'We just had a meal at his friend's restaurant.'

'And then?'

'And then he walked me home.'

'Did he kiss you?' Julie asked.

'What makes you think he would've kissed me?' Kitty asked.

'He's a man.'

'I'd rather not talk about it.'

'So he *did* kiss you,' Julie said. 'How was it?'

'I told you I'm not going to talk about it.'

'I bet it was completely different from Charles.'

'I'm not listening,' she said in a singsong tone.

'Are you going to see him again?' Julie asked.

'I can hardly avoid it when he works at the same hospital, can I?'

'I mean see him as in *see* him.'

Kitty thought of how distant and formal Jake had been the other night at the hospital. It had been a stark turnaround from the intimate exchange they had shared. It was as if he had regretted talking to her about his family circumstances and his brother's situation in particular. He had lowered his guard just long enough for her to glimpse some of his pain and frustration, but he had snapped the drawbridge back up as soon as he could, locking her out. He was prepared to offer her a no-strings relationship but not access to the innermost yearnings of his heart.

'Jake Chandler isn't really interested in me other than as a one-off affair,' she said. 'I haven't been around the block enough times for him. He likes his women casual and carefree.'

'You mark my words,' Julie said. 'It's the cynical ones who always fall for sweet, homespun girls like you. But anyway, why shouldn't you have a little fling with him while you're here? Isn't it time you had a bit of fun? You spent years and years with the same guy, for God's sake. For years you've acted like an old married lady. But you're single now. You can do what you want with whoever you want. This is your chance to let your hair down a bit. Live a little. Put yourself out there. You're only twenty-six. There'll be plenty of time for settling down with Mr Right later on. What have you got to lose?'

'I don't want to get hurt,' Kitty said.

'You take life way too seriously, Kitty-Kat,' Julie said. 'You always have. You're allowed to have sex without being in love with someone, you know. And you don't need a ring on your finger, either.'

Kitty looked at the promise ring that was too tight on her hand. Was it time to put the past aside and do as her cousin said?

Kitty was on her way to her first practice session with the combined hospitals doctors' orchestra she had been invited to join when her car refused to start. The engine coughed and spluttered and then died. She turned the key again, but this time there was only a clicking sound— and a faint one at that.

'I don't believe this,' she muttered. 'Why are you doing this to me now?'

A shadow blocked out the driver's side window. 'Need any help?' Jake asked.

She clenched her hands on the steering wheel

and stared straight ahead. 'If you're going to say "I told you so", then please don't.'

'Wouldn't dream of it.'

She blew out a breath and threw him a frustrated glance. 'I can't get my car to start.'

'Want me to have a look?'

'Be my guest,' she said, cranking open the driver's door. She squeezed out past him, her body tingling where it brushed against his in the confined space between her car and the wall.

He sat in the driver's seat and turned on the ignition while his foot gave the throttle a couple of pumps. 'Sounds like a blockage in the fuel line.' He leaned down and popped the bonnet lever. 'I'll have a quick look under the hood.'

Kitty sucked in her tummy as he moved past her. He looked so vital and male dressed in a black T-shirt and chinos. Every muscle looked as if it had been carved to his torso by a master sculptor. He smelt like summer—a mixture of surf and sweat, sunscreen and aftershave. She wanted to run her hands down the muscular slope of his back and shoulders, to press her mouth to his and feel him shudder with need.

Maybe her cousin was right. What would be so wrong about indulging her senses for once? What harm would there be in a relationship with him, even if it was on his terms? Wasn't it time she lived a little? It wasn't as if she had to be as progressive as her parents. Even a short-term relationship could be exclusive. She wouldn't settle for anything less. It was just so tempting to explore the chemistry she shared with Jake. What if she never felt this level of excitement again? She would regret it for the rest of her life. She would spend the rest of her days wondering what she'd missed out on. She would have no memories of his possession. No images in her head of their bodies entwined in passion. Her body would never know the full extent of its sensual response in his arms.

She *wanted* to know.

'Want to give it another try?' Jake called out.

Kitty snapped out of her reverie and turned the ignition. The engine choked and spluttered and then died. 'Am I doing something wrong?' she asked.

'No,' he said, coming round to her side as he

wiped his hands on a handkerchief. 'The fuel line was definitely blocked but it sounds like your battery's had it as well. I can hook it up to my charger overnight.'

'But I have to get to my practice session,' she said, frowning at him in worry. 'I've joined a local doctors' orchestra. It's our first session to-night.'

'I can give you a lift.'

Kitty gnawed at her lip. 'What if people see me getting out of your car?'

A smile lifted the edges of his mouth. 'I prom-ise not to kiss you goodbye, OK?'

She gave him a guarded look. 'How do I know if I can trust you on that?' she asked.

His sapphire-blue gaze flicked to her mouth for a heartbeat. 'You can't,' he said, and then turned and led the way to his car.

Jake pulled up outside the church hall where the orchestra was rehearsing in the suburb of Annandale on the other side of the city. 'How long will you be?' he asked.

'You don't have to wait for me,' Kitty said. 'I'll

get one of the other doctors to drop me off near a bus stop or a cab rank.'

'I don't mind waiting,' he said, putting on the handbrake. 'Even better, why don't I come in and listen?'

'It's probably not to your taste.'

He gave her a sardonic smile. 'A little too high-brow for someone like me, huh?'

She tightened her mouth. 'I didn't say that.'

'I've heard about this orchestra but I've never been to any of their concerts,' he said. 'Maybe it's time I stretched my horizons a bit.'

'Please don't feel you have to do so on my account,' she said. 'I'm quite happy to make my own arrangements.'

He got out of the car and came around to open her door for her. 'I've got nothing better to do this evening,' he said.

Kitty tried to concentrate on the conductor's beat but her gaze kept drifting to where Jake was sitting in the stalls. He kept smiling at her in that indolent way of his, making her fingers fumble over the notes like a nervous schoolgirl at her first school concert. But about halfway through the rehearsal she noticed him glance at his phone. It must have been important because he got up and left the hall and it was at least ten or fifteen minutes before he came back.

'That's it, everyone,' the conductor said as the session drew to an end. 'Same time next week if you can make it.'

Kitty made her way to where Jake was chatting to a couple of the doctors he had introduced her to earlier. 'Thanks for waiting,' she said, once they had moved on. 'I hope you weren't too bored.'

'Not at all,' he said. 'I found it relaxing. I had no idea you could play like that.'

'I'm not that good,' she said. 'I need to do much more practice.'

'Well, from my end it certainly didn't sound as if any cats were being tortured.'

She gave him a sideways glance. 'Thanks.'

'How long have you been playing?'

'I started when I was six,' she said. 'My parents wanted me to experiment with a whole range of instruments, but I only ever wanted to play the violin. I finally wore them down.'

He gave her a crooked smile as he led the way out to the car. 'Not many kids nag their parents to learn a classical instrument,' he said. 'Isn't it normally the other way around?'

'I know,' Kitty said wryly. 'I think I'm a throw-back. My parents are quite ashamed of me for being so conservative. I haven't got a single piercing or a tattoo. I don't even dye my hair.'

'Why would you want to?' he said. 'It's fine the way it is.'

'It's boring.'

He stopped, reaching out and picking up a stray lock of her hair. He coiled it around his finger. 'It's not boring,' he said. 'It's beautiful—especially when it's loose like this.'

Kitty felt the voltage of his touch all the way down the shafts of her hair to the skin of her sensitive scalp. The skin on her body tingled in sharpened awareness as he came that little bit closer.

Her breasts tightened behind her clothes.

Her breath stalled in her throat.

Her pulse rate escalated.

Her mind turned to mush.

The warm fragrant night air cast its spell of seduction around her, making her forget everything but the way his mouth had felt on hers. She felt the hard tug of attraction deep in the pit of her belly, pulling her towards his body like a magnet does a tiny iron filing.

'I should get you home,' he said as he stepped back from her.

'Yes…I've taken up far too much of your time as it is.'

Kitty was acutely aware of him sitting so close to her inside the confines of his car. Her gaze kept tracking to his tanned arm as it worked the gear shift. And his muscular thigh as it bunched and released when he pressed down on the clutch. She imagined those muscles in the throes of passion. She imagined those hands exploring her body, touching her in places that made the breath hitch in her throat. She remembered the intimate stroke of his tongue and wondered what it would feel like to have it lick and stroke her breasts or between her thighs. She had never felt comfortable enough to allow Charles to explore her so intimately. But somehow she sensed that nothing would be off-limits to Jake Chandler. He would be a masterful and exciting lover—and a demanding one. She had felt it in that disturbingly erotic kiss. Her body had responded with such fervency to the head-spinning experience of his mouth commandeering hers. It had probably been just another kiss to him, but to her it had been a revelation. It had shown her how out of control her needs could be given the right inducement.

She had never thought of herself as a particularly passionate person. She had put her lacklustre love-life with Charles down to a mixture of long-term familiarity and the exhausting demands of their careers. But in Jake Chandler's arms she had been transformed into a wild woman with even wilder needs. She thought again of what would happen if she gave in to those needs. So many young women her age enjoyed casual flings. It was part of life these days. She was becoming a bit of an anachronism with her white picket fence and pram mentality. Why couldn't she have the same freedom as other girls her age? It wasn't as if she had to fall in love with him. He was hardly likely to fall in love with her. Could she be brave enough to step out of her comfort zone and live a little?

Jake's phone rang and he answered it via the Bluetooth device on the steering wheel. 'Jake Chandler.'

'Hi, Jake, it's Tiffany. Remember me?'

'Tiffany...' He scratched his jaw. 'From the gym, right?'

The woman gave a tinkling laugh. 'That's the one,' she said. 'Are you up for a drink some time?'

Kitty rolled her eyes and looked out of the window, a fist of jealousy clutching at her insides. What a silly fool she had been to think he would wait patiently for her to make up her mind.

*Of course he wouldn't wait.*

He probably had a waiting list of potential lovers. She was just a temporary diversion from his usual list of candidates. Her temporary appointment at St Benedict's gave him a perfect get-out clause—a three-month affair with no strings.

'Yeah, why not?' Jake was saying. 'How about tomorrow at Brad's place? Shall we say around nine?'

'Lovely,' the woman said. 'I'll look forward to it.'

'See you then, Tiffany,' he said. *'Ciao.'*

Kitty threw him a look of disgust. 'You could have at least waited until I was out of the car before you planned your next seduction.'

'We're just meeting for a drink,' he said.

'You don't even remember who she is, do you?'

'I can picture her,' he said, frowning as if trying to recall. 'Blonde hair, long legs, nice smile.'

'Have you slept with her?'

'Not yet.'

Kitty's insides clenched again. 'What's stopping you?'

'There's the little matter of a thousand bucks, for one thing,' he said. 'I'm not going to lose a bet like that unless I'm sure it's going to be worth it.'

Did he think *she* would be worth it? Kitty

wondered. Could it be possible that he found her just as exciting and tempting as she found him? It had certainly felt that way while he was kissing her. She had felt the powerful charge of his desire. His body had left an imprint on hers she could feel even now.

'And the other thing is I like to be the one who does the chasing,' he added.

'Isn't that a little old fashioned of you?'

He flashed her a quick grin as he swung his car into the car park. 'Look who's talking, Miss Nineteenth Century.'

As soon as the car drew to a halt Kitty opened the passenger door. 'Thank you for taking me,' she said stiffly. 'I hope I didn't disrupt your plans for tonight too much.'

'It was fine,' he said. 'I enjoyed myself.'

'Goodnight.'

He waved a hand. ''Night.'

# CHAPTER TEN

'STUPID, stupid, *stupid*,' Kitty berated herself as she cleansed her face in her bathroom a few minutes later. 'What were you thinking?' She grabbed a bunch of tissues and savagely wiped off her cleanser. 'Miss Nineteenth Century. What a jerk!'

The doorbell sounded.

Kitty tossed the tissues in the bin and went down to open the door—to find Jake standing there with her violin case.

'You forgot something,' he said, holding the case out to her.

'Oh...' She took it from him with a sheepish look. 'Thanks.'

'I called my mate about your car,' he said. 'I told him I'd drop it off at his workshop once I get the battery charged.'

'Thank you, but I don't want to put you to any more trouble.'

'No problem,' he said.

Kitty went to close the door but he put a foot out to stop it from closing. 'Aren't you going to ask me in for a coffee or something?' he asked.

'I'm sure you've had much better offers this evening,' she said with a speaking look.

'Phone's been running hot, but I thought I'd have a quiet one tonight.'

'Good for you.' She pushed against the door again. 'Do you mind?'

His gaze ran over her teddy bear pyjamas. 'Am I keeping you out of bed?'

'Not at all,' she said. 'It's not even eleven o'clock.'

'Then let's have a nightcap,' he said. 'You owe me one for driving you all that way tonight.'

She stepped back from the door. 'You said it wasn't a problem.'

'It wasn't. But then I found your violin case. The least you could do is offer me a drink for delivering it to your door.'

She blew out a breath of resignation. 'What would you like?' she asked.

'What are you having?'

Kitty hoped he couldn't see the milk and choc-chip cookies she had laid out on the table for her supper. 'I was thinking about a glass of wine,' she said, surreptitiously blocking his view of the kitchen. 'Do you like red or white?'

'What have you got open?'

'Nothing as yet,' she said. 'I'm not a big drinker.'

'Then don't open anything on my account.'

'I have a bottle of red one of the patients gave me,' she said. 'They dropped it off the other day.'

'It's nice when they do that,' he said. 'We patch them up and move them on, but now and again someone recognises what we actually do.'

Kitty handed him a glass of the wine. 'It's one of the downsides of working in A&E,' she said. 'We only see them the once and they move on.'

'I think it's one of the good sides,' he said. 'You don't have to get too involved.'

She studied him for a moment as he took a sip of his wine. 'Your professional life has a lot in common with your private one,' she said. 'Both are full of brief encounters where no feelings get involved.'

'Works for me.'

'Don't you get tired of that sea of nameless faces coming and going in your life?'

He took another measured sip of his wine. 'Nope.'

'But it's so selfish and…and so pointless,' she said. 'How can you not feel something for the women you sleep with?'

One of his shoulders rose and fell in an off-hand shrug. 'Guess I'm not built that way.'

'So it's just sex,' she said with a disparaging look. 'Nothing more than inserting Item A in Slot B.'

His mouth tilted. 'I have a little more finesse than your charming description allows,' he said. 'But then, perhaps your own experience has somewhat limited your outlook.'

Kitty felt a blush steal over her face and neck. 'I have enough experience to know that sex is not just a physical connection,' she said. 'It's a deeply emotional experience.'

'Clearly your boyfriend didn't find it so emotionally satisfying, otherwise why did he find someone else?'

She threw him an arctic glare. 'I think it might be time for you to leave.'

He held her look with a cynical glitter in his eye. 'You need to grow up, Kitty,' he said. 'You're a young, fanciful girl in a woman's body. Life isn't a fairytale. There are no handsome princes out there who'll declare undying love for you and carry you off into the sunset. There are no fairy godmothers to make everything turn out right in the end. There are no genies in bottles, no magic spells, and sure as hell there are precious few happy ever afters.'

Kitty folded her arms imperiously. 'Are you done?'

The air crackled with electric tension as dark blue eyes warred with grey.

'No,' he said, eyes glittering as he closed the distance between them in one stride. 'Not quite.'

She took a step backwards as he came towards her but the sofa was in the way. She gave a little startled gasp as his strong hands gripped her by the upper arms, pulling her to him. Her body jolted with sensual energy when it came into contact with his. It was like a dead battery being plugged into a power source. Currents of energy flowed through her, kick-starting her senses into throbbing, pulsing life. His mouth came down and blazed with furnace-hot heat against hers. As the kiss progressed in intensity raw need licked along her flesh like trails of runaway fire. Desire pooled in her belly, hot and liquid, melting her to the backbone. His tongue thrust boldly into her mouth, commanding and conquering, demanding and deliciously, dangerously male.

For a moment, a mere nanosecond, she thought about resisting. But the feel of his tongue weaving seductively around hers was her undoing. She wound her arms around his neck, leaning into his kiss, giving back, responding in an unabashed way she wouldn't have believed possible just a few days ago. Red-hot need rose in her like a hungry beast waking after a long hibernation. It roared from deep within her, great primal bellows of unmet wants that refused to be ignored and denied or suppressed any longer.

Her fingers delved deep into the thick pelt of his hair. His hard chest wall abraded her breasts as she pressed herself closer and closer. She felt the swelling ridge of his erection against her feminine mound, a tantalising reminder of his power and strength and her primitive need to yield to it.

One of his hands pressed against the small of her back and the other went to her hair, his fingers splaying against her scalp as he kissed her deeply and urgently.

Her tongue played cat and mouse with his. She brazenly teased and tantalised him with darting, flicking movements of her own. He took control back from her with another shift in position. His hand went from her hair to her breast, cupping it possessively, his palm moulding its contour with sensual expertise.

Kitty was breathless with escalating need. She hadn't realised her breasts could feel quite so sensitive. The nipples were tight, and aching for more of his touch. As if he read her mind, or indeed her body, he glided his hand up under her pyjama top and captured her naked breast.

Lightning bolts of desire zapped through her body at that shamelessly intimate contact. Her nipple budded into his palm; she felt the delicious pressure and wanted more. His thumb moved over the tight nub, back and forth in a mesmerising motion that set every nerve singing.

And then, most shocking of all, he bent his head and took her nipple and its areola into his hot, moist mouth. She clung to him as the world spun, soft little whimpers coming from deep inside her throat as his tongue stroked her into mindlessness.

He moved to her other breast, taking his time over exploring it, teasing it with his teeth and tongue. A shiver scuttled over her flesh—how could her body not have known such exquisite pleasure existed? How could she not have felt such earth-shattering sensations before?

He worked his way back to her mouth, lingering over the sensitive skin of her neck until he claimed her lips once more. This kiss had an undercurrent of desperation to it. She felt his need building, a rampage of want that thundered through his blood. She felt the potent power of him surging against her body. It awoke a primal need inside her to open to him. Her body pulsed and vibrated with a longing so intense it made a mockery of anything she had experienced before. She had never felt such powerful, all-consuming desire. It took over every thought. It blocked out every resistance. It was as if he had unlocked a part of her being she hadn't known existed.

How could it be *her* hands greedily seeking his naked chest underneath his T-shirt?

How could it be *her* mouth responding to his with such reckless abandon?

How could *her* body be rubbing up against his like a shameless wanton?

Suddenly it was over.

He put her from him almost roughly. 'What the hell do you think you're doing?'

Kitty took umbrage at his attitude. 'Me?' she asked. 'You started it!'

He raked a hand through his disordered hair, his breathing still heavy and uneven. 'I know, and now I've stopped it,' he said.

She crossed her arms over her chest. 'I would have stopped it before it went too much further.'

His eyes were like a laser as they held hers. 'You were taking your merry time about it, sweetheart.'

Kitty shot him an icy glare. 'You caught me off guard. It's late and I'm tired and not thinking straight.'

His lip curled mockingly. 'Still think sex is all about emotion?'

She felt her cheeks radiate with colour. 'We didn't have sex.'

'We weren't far off it.'

'I would *never* have let you make love to me.'

He came up close again, capturing her chin between his thumb and forefinger, his eyes holding hers in a hot, tense little lockdown that sent a shudder of reaction all the way down her spine. 'I could've had you flat on your back and screaming all the way to heaven and back and you damn well know it,' he said.

Kitty felt the echo of his incendiary statement deep in the pit of her belly. She wanted to make him take those shamelessly coarse words back. God help her, she wanted those shamelessly coarse words *not* to have a grain of truth in them.

She wrenched out of his hold, rubbing at her chin as if it had been stung. 'You are a loathsome, diabolical, arrogant man,' she said through gritted teeth. 'I detest men like you. You think you can have any woman you want, any time you want, but you can't. You can't have *me*.'

His mouth still had that slant of mockery in place. 'You really shouldn't have thrown down such a delightful little gauntlet,' he said. 'Now I'll have to prove you wrong.'

She held herself stiffly: arms folded, back straight, mouth tight. 'You'd be wasting your time.'

'I don't know about that,' he said as his gaze ran over her indolently. 'It'd sure be fun trying.'

Kitty glowered at him. 'What about your bet?'

'Some rules are made to be broken,' he said. 'Anyway, everyone already thinks we're doing it. Why not do it for real?'

'I'd rather die.'

'You're afraid, aren't you?' he asked. 'You're

afraid of being out of your depth in a relation-ship. That's why you chose a boyfriend you'd known for ages. He was safe and predictable. You could control things with him. But that's not what you need.'

'I hardly think you're the person to tell me what I need,' she tossed back. 'You barely know me.'

'I know you well enough to know that be-hind that starchy schoolmistress thing you've got going on is a young woman who longs to let her hair down,' he said.

Kitty gave a scathing little laugh. 'And I sup-pose you think you're exactly the person I should let it down with? Thanks, but no thanks.'

He strode across to the door. 'Let me know if you change your mind,' he said. 'You know where to find me.'

# CHAPTER ELEVEN

'WHAT'S wrong with this place?' Julie asked outside Brad's bar and grill the following evening, when they were scouting for somewhere to have dinner.

'I'm not going in *there*,' Kitty said, turning up her nose.

'What's wrong with it? It looks nice, and they have live music.'

'It's a pick-up joint,' Kitty said. 'Let's go somewhere more sophisticated.'

'But I'm thirty and I'm single,' Julie wailed. 'I *need* a pick-up joint.'

'Well, *I* don't.

'You're single too,' Julie said. 'Or has that changed since we last spoke?'

'I hate men,' Kitty said, scowling. 'They're so shallow and selfish.'

'I know, but that's part of the attraction,' Julie

said. 'We're so giving and selfless. It's that whole opposites attract thing. Hey, isn't that your boss?'

Kitty put her head down. 'Keep moving,' she said. 'We'll find another place further along.'

'God, he's even hotter than I remembered,' Julie said. 'Maybe he'll join us. Why don't you invite him?'

'He already has plans,' Kitty said, tugging at Julie's arm. *'Come on.'*

Julie shrugged off Kitty's hand. 'I'm going to thank him for checking me out,' she said. 'I should've thought to drop in a bottle of wine or something. I bet he would've appreciated that.'

'He wouldn't have remembered who you were,' Kitty muttered.

'Hi,' Julie said as she blocked Jake from moving any further along the footpath. 'I'm Kitty's cousin. You saw me in A&E a few days ago.'

'How could I forget?' Jake said with a smile. 'How's the ankle?'

'I'm off the crutches, as you can see,' Julie said. 'How is Kitty shaping up?'

'She's proving to be quite an asset to the team,'

he said. 'We wonder now how we managed without her.'

Kitty glowered at him. 'We mustn't keep you,' she said. 'Come on, Julie. Dr Chandler has an important date.'

'She cancelled,' Jake said.

'How dreadfully disappointing for you,' Kitty said.

'You win some, you lose some,' he said with a dismissive shrug. 'Plenty more fish in the sea.'

'So you're putting your line out again this evening?' Kitty asked with a pert look. 'Good luck with that.'

He smiled a lazy smile. 'What about you?' he asked. 'A hot night on the town?'

'I wish,' Julie said, rolling her eyes. 'Why don't you join us?'

'I'm sure Dr Chandler has much better things to do than keep us company,' Kitty said.

'I'd love to join you, but I'm meeting someone,' he said.

Kitty curled her lip. 'That was quick.'

'Yeah,' he said. 'Nothing like the right bait. Works like a charm.'

Kitty looped her arm through her cousin's. 'Don't let us keep you.'

'What was all that about?' Julie asked when they had walked on a bit.

'What do you mean?'

'You were spitting chips at each other,' Julie said. 'I could've cut the air with a knife.'

'That man has a revolving door on his bedroom,' Kitty said in disgust. 'He's the biggest playboy imaginable. He had the gall to set up one of his shallow hook-ups while I was sitting right beside him in the car.'

'What were you doing beside him in his car?'

'It's a long story.'

'Tell me.'

'He took me to my orchestra rehearsal,' she said. 'My car broke down.'

'That was nice of him.'

'He only did it to rub my nose in it.'

'What do you mean?' Julie asked.

'He gave me a lecture about buying second-hand cars,' Kitty said. 'Honestly, you'd think I'd committed a crime. And that was on top of the dressing down he gave me about water restrictions. How was I to know you're not supposed to use a hose to wash your car?'

'I should've told you about that—sorry.'

'It's not *your* fault.'

'It's not his fault, either.'

'Yes, it is,' Kitty said. 'He just loves to lord it over me. He doesn't like the way I pay attention to detail at work. But I don't have his depth of experience or confidence. I can't just waltz in and diagnose everyone just like that. I need to feel my way.'

'I'm sure he's only trying to help you,' Julie said. 'He seemed quite positive about your being a part of the team when I asked him.'

'He doesn't think I'm up to the task,' Kitty said. 'He thinks I'm scared of being out of my depth.'

'But you are,' Julie said. 'It's what I was telling you the other day. You're a classic control freak. Sooner or later you're going to have to realise you can't control everything in life. Anyway, how boring would that be?'

'I'm perfectly happy with my life the way it is,' Kitty said.

'I wish I could say the same,' Julie said wistfully. 'I wonder if I'll ever meet someone who wants the same things I do.'

Kitty squeezed her cousin's hand. 'That's the fairytale, isn't it? We have to believe, otherwise what hope is there?'

Jake checked his watch yet again. It wasn't the first time his brother had stood him up. He had been left waiting on numerous occasions, but he could never bring himself to leave until he was absolutely sure Robbie wasn't going to show. He always gave him a chance to redeem himself. The psychologists would probably call it enabling behaviour, but what else could he do? Robbie was his flesh and blood. He hated to think of him out on the streets, desperate for food or shelter. He had to do what he could to protect him.

'Got a dollar, mate?' A voice spoke from a bundle of rags on the sidewalk.

Jake fished in his pocket for some money. 'Why are you on the streets?' he asked, dropping the coins in the tin.

'Got nowhere else to go,' the man said, quickly pocketing the money.

'What about shelters?'

'Cost money.'

'What about your family?'

'Don't have no family.'

'Everyone has family,' Jake said.

'Not me,' the guy said. 'You?'

'Yeah,' Jake said. 'They drive me nuts.'

'That's what families do.'

Jake took out his wallet and peeled off a few notes. 'Here,' he said, handing them to him. 'Find yourself a hotel or something. Don't blow it on drugs or drink.'

Kitty padded out to her kitchen early the following morning for a glass of water before her shower. She pulled up the blind on the kitchen window and saw Jake in his own kitchen on the opposite side of the courtyard. He was standing in front of his open refrigerator—and he was naked.

Her eyes drank in the sight of him, all bronzed and buffed, every muscle toned and taut with good health and vigour. He looked as if he had just stepped off a marble plinth in a museum. Not a gram of fat on him anywhere, just strong lean planes of hard male flesh.

She gave a little gulp.

He closed the fridge and turned and saw her staring at him. A slow smile spread over his features. He raised the carton of juice he was holding in a salute and mouthed, *Good morning.*

Kitty pulled the blind back down with more haste than efficiency. She clutched the edge of the sink, breathing hard. What must he think of her, gawping at him like that? Had he done it on purpose? Did he make a habit of wandering around naked in full view of the neighbours? So what if she was the only neighbour residing here just now—he had no right to flaunt himself like that!

Then she remembered his hot little hook-up. He probably had *her* there, still lying languorously in his bed after a bed-wrecking night of sex.

She stomped off to the shower, but as the water flowed over her in stinging little needles she thought of him having a shower next door, no doubt sharing it with his lover. Was he soaping up her breasts? Was he kissing her neck and décolletage?

'*Grrrrggh.*' Kitty reached for a towel and scrubbed herself dry. 'I hate that man!'

Kitty was on her way to her car to drive to work when she remembered Jake had arranged to deliver it to his mate's workshop. Just as she was about to call a cab on her mobile, he appeared from round the corner.

'Want a lift?' he asked.

Kitty couldn't control her fiery blush. 'Please don't put yourself out any further,' she said. 'I can easily call a cab.'

'At this time of the morning?' he said. 'It's bedlam out there. I just fought my way through it with your heap of rust. Only just made it too. I think the radiator's about to go on it as well.'

'I'm sorry you've had such a trying start to the morning,' she said.

His dark blue eyes glinted. 'My morning started out just fine.'

Kitty opened the passenger door and bundled herself inside, cheeks still burning hot. Did he have to embarrass her even further?

'How did your night on the town go?' he asked once he was behind the wheel.

She threw him a flinty look. 'It was probably excruciatingly tedious compared to yours.'

'I don't know about that,' he said, checking for traffic as he pulled into the street. 'I've had better.'

Kitty glanced at him but his expression was unfathomable. 'Are you going to see her again?' she asked.

'Who?'

'Your hot date last night.'

He changed lanes before he answered. 'Maybe. It depends.'

'On what?'

He glanced at her wryly. 'Why the sudden interest? Are you thinking of joining the queue?'

'Don't be daft,' she scoffed.

His mouth slanted in a smile. 'Frightened you might get trampled in the rush?'

Kitty pressed her lips together and refused to

say another word until he pulled into the hospital car park. 'Thank you for the lift,' she said.

'I'd offer to run you home again, but I have another commitment straight after work,' he said.

'I'll make my own arrangements,' she said.

'Here's my mate's card,' he said, reaching for a business card from one of the dashboard compartments. 'You can give him a call to find out when your car will be ready.'

Kitty felt the brush of his fingers as he handed her the card and her belly gave a little flutter. 'Thanks...'

His eyes meshed with hers, dark and intense and *knowing*.

Could he feel the sexual energy she could feel? Did it make his skin ache to feel her touch? Did his lips tingle at the memory of hers moving against them? Did his blood roar through his veins at the thought of holding her in his arms, moulding her to him, *making love* to her?

'I like how you had your hair this morning,' he said.

Kitty put a hand up to her neat chignon. 'My... hair?'

'First thing,' he said. 'It was down and all tousled. That just-out-of-bed look really suits you.'

'You caught me by surprise.'

He gave her an indolent smile. 'Ditto.'

'I'm going to work,' she said, swinging her bag over her shoulder. 'I'll see you inside.'

# CHAPTER TWELVE

'Was that Jake Chandler's car I saw you getting out of this morning?' Cathy Oxley asked in the locker room.

Kitty put her bag in the locker and closed the door. 'He gave me a lift to work as my car is being repaired.'

'What is going on with you two?' Cathy asked. 'One of the doctors from Paediatrics said Jake took you to an orchestra rehearsal. Are you or aren't you an item?'

'Nothing's going on,' Kitty said. 'Dr Chandler kindly offered to take me to the rehearsal at short notice when my car refused to start. He also kindly offered to deliver my car to his friend's workshop.'

'Why would he do that if he wasn't interested in you?'

'He was just being neighbourly.'

'Some people have all the luck,' Cathy said. 'All my neighbour does is complain about my cat or my kids.'

'I'm not Dr Chandler's type,' Kitty said. 'Apparently I don't let my hair down enough.'

'Did he say that to you?'

Kitty compressed her lips. 'Amongst other things.'

Cathy grinned. 'I think he likes you. I've seen the way he looks at you. He sure as hell doesn't look at anyone else like that.'

'He has a different lover every night,' Kitty said, scowling furiously. 'He probably doesn't have time to look at them before he shoves them out the door again.'

'You know it's the hardened playboys who always fall for the old-fashioned girls in the long run,' Cathy said. 'I've seen it many a time.'

'You won't be seeing it this time,' Kitty said as they walked out of the locker room together. 'I've never met a more irritating, beastly, odious man.'

'Er...' Cathy gave a grimace. 'I've got to go. See you.'

Kitty turned around to see Jake Chandler standing there with an inscrutable look on his face.

'Haven't you got better things to do than discuss me with the nursing staff?' he asked.

She stood her ground. 'I'm trying to put out the rumours that are circulating about us,' she said. 'I thought if everyone knew how much I hated you it would stop them speculating.'

'Hate is a strong word, Dr Cargill.'

She refused to be intimidated by his steely gaze. 'I know,' she said. 'But it's appropriate in this case.'

'I have a feeling you don't hate me as much as you'd like to,' he said. 'I threaten you. That's what you hate, isn't it, Kitty? I make you feel things you don't want to feel. You don't want to feel desire, do you? It frightens the hell out of you.'

Kitty glowered at him. 'I don't feel any such thing.'

'Sure you do, sweetheart,' he drawled. 'You want me. You want me real bad.'

'You're mistaken,' she said, her heart racing, her breath catching.

He captured her wrist in his strong fingers, his thumb finding her pounding pulse. 'This is what I do to you, isn't it?' he asked. 'It's the same thing you do to me.'

Kitty swallowed again, her stomach plummeting when she saw the naked desire in his gaze. She felt the sensual pull of his body, and the heat and fire of his touch set off every nerve screaming for more.

She *was* frightened by how he made her feel. Frightened and yet exhilarated.

'Dr Chandler?' One of the residents approached from further down the corridor.

Jake dropped Kitty's wrist and turned around. 'Yes?'

The resident looked from Kitty to Jake. 'I'm sorry to interrupt…'

'You're not interrupting anything,' Jake said, dropping his hand by his side.

'There's a patient just come in who keeps asking for you,' the intern said. 'He says he's your brother.'

Jake went to Bay Two, where Robbie was lying groaning on the trolley. It angered him to see his younger brother so wasted at this time of the day. His skin looked grey and pasty and his hair looked as if it hadn't been washed in a week. His clothes were little more than filthy rags and his shoes had holes in them. How had his kid brother got to this? What choices had he made that had sent him on this crazy, sense-less trajectory? Why couldn't he just turn his life around? Did he have no self-control or self-respect? Didn't he want things to be different? How could he expect to live a full life when he was abusing his health so wilfully?

'Isn't it a bit early for a hangover?' he said as he twitched the curtain closed. 'Or is this one left over from last night?'

Robbie clutched at his head. 'Don't talk so loud.'

'You know, if you're here for a hand-out there are much better ways to do it.' Jake said. 'I told you I'd pay for rent and food. You don't have to use emotional blackmail.'

'I'm sick, damn it,' Robbie said.

'Yeah, well, I would be too if I was on the same liquid diet you're on,' Jake said. 'When was the last time you had a proper meal?'

'I don't know…couple of days ago, I think.'

'Perhaps I should assess him?' Kitty said. 'I'm not family. I can be a bit more objective.'

Jake fought with himself. He was used to handling his family issues on his own. He didn't want the train wreck of his brother's issues to intersect with his professional life. It wasn't only that it was embarrassing. He felt so damned helpless. He was used to sorting out other people's problems. His life was devoted to saving other people's sons and daughters, brothers and sisters, mothers and fathers, and yet he couldn't do a thing to put his kid brother's life back on track.

'Go for it,' he said. 'You won't find anything but a chip on his shoulder.'

Kitty stepped forward. 'Hello, Robbie.'

'Don't listen to him,' Robbie said. 'I *am* sick. I know I am.'

'What have you been doing to yourself?' Kitty asked as she examined him. 'Can you open both eyes for me? Yes, that's right. Sorry the light is so bright.'

'My head is killing me.'

'Have you had a recent fall?' she asked.

'I've had a few falls lately,' Robbie said.

'Excessive amounts of alcohol will do that,' Jake put in sardonically.

Kitty gave him a quelling look before turning back to his brother. 'How many falls?' she asked.

Robbie frowned. 'I can't remember...two, maybe three in the last twenty-four hours.'

'Did you know you were falling, or did it happen so fast you had no warning?' Kitty asked, examining his pupils again.

'I just found myself on the ground with no idea how I got there,' Robbie said.

'Do you take any medication?' Kitty asked. 'Prescription or otherwise?'

'Not for a while,' Robbie said. 'I used to smoke dope. I stopped a few months back.'

'Nothing else?'

'No,' Robbie said. 'I have the odd drink but I'm trying to cut back a bit. I don't like how it makes me feel any more.'

'So it feels different when you drink now from how it felt before?' Kitty asked.

'It just takes more to get him drunk than it did before,' Jake muttered.

Kitty threw him another gnarly look. 'Do you mind?' she asked.

'He's my brother.'

Her eyes flashed grey lightning. 'He's *my* patient.'

Jake twitched aside the curtains. 'I'll leave you to him,' he said. 'I have better things to do with my time than try and help people who won't even lift a finger to help themselves.'

Kitty put a hand on Robbie's shoulder. 'Sorry about that,' she said.

Robbie put a hand over his closed eyes.

Kitty sat on the edge of the bed trolley. 'Do you want to talk about it?'

He shook his head, and then grimaced as if the movement had caused him pain. 'Not much point, is there? Nothing's going to change. I've stuffed everything up.'

'It's not too late to turn things around.'

He turned his head on the pillow and cranked open one bloodshot eye. 'You think?'

She covered his thin hand with hers. 'Jake's concerned about you.'

He gave a grunt as he laid his head back down and closed his eyes. 'Jake needs to get a life.'

'Maybe he can't do that until he feels you're on the right track,' Kitty said.

A muscle ticked in Robbie's jaw, which reminded Kitty of Jake so much she felt a little ache settle around her heart.

'I'm not doing this on purpose,' he said.

'Sometimes it's hard to see that from the outside,' Kitty said. 'The effort you put in might not seem like much effort at all from Jake's perspective.'

Robbie put his wrist across his forehead and closed his eyes. 'I don't know why I'm like this,' he said. 'I just can't seem to get my life sorted out.'

'There are people who can help you with that,' she said. 'Psychologists, counsellors, even a life coach can help you put steps in place to get back on your feet.'

'I'm not going to a shrink,' Robbie said, dropping his arm back down on the bed. 'They just put you on drugs and bomb you out.'

'Not always,' Kitty said. 'If there's a mental health issue that needs to be addressed, then certainly one way of managing it is drug therapy, but there are other options.'

'I'm not a nut case,' Robbie said scowling at her.

'Then let's see if there is something else going on, shall we?' Kitty said. 'I'm going to run a couple of tests to check your blood count and thyroid and kidney function to start with. Have you had any recent tests done? Blood? Scans? That sort of thing?'

He looked away. 'Jake ordered some tests a while back,' he mumbled.

'Are the results with your GP, or did Jake deal with it directly?' Kitty asked.

'He doesn't usually treat me or my sisters,' Robbie said. 'He'll write the occasional script but he prefers us to have our own GP.'

'Did anything come up?'

Robbie looked sheepish. 'I only had a blood

test done. When Jake asked me about the scan he ordered I told him it'd been clear.'

Kitty wondered why Robbie's GP hadn't formally written to Jake to inform him of the results, as per the usual protocol. But on questioning Robbie further she found out that he had been attending a large and busy medical clinic and had not seen the same practitioner twice. Perhaps Jake had been satisfied another colleague was taking over the care of his brother and had left it at that.

Kitty took blood from Robbie's arm and popped the vials in the appropriate bags ready for pathology. She turned back to look at him and frowned when she noticed one of his eyes was twitching.

'How long have you had that twitch?' she asked.

He blinked a couple of times. 'Couple of days…maybe more.'

Kitty examined both his pupils again. Now the left one was slightly more dilated. 'Those falls you said you had,' she said. 'Did you hit your head at all?'

'Not that I can remember,' he said. 'I haven't got a bump, or anything, just the mother of all headaches.'

'I think I'll order a scan to be on the safe side,' she said. 'Then we'll take it from there.'

Jake came out of Cubicle Eight after seeing a patient with a gall bladder attack as Kitty came past. 'How's my brother doing?' he asked. 'Have you convinced him to check in to rehab?'

She stood before him, her expression sombre. 'I'm sending him for a CT scan.'

'You're wasting your time,' he said. 'I sent him for one a few months back. Nothing showed up.'

'He didn't have it done,' she said. 'There's no scan in the system. I checked. I even rang the clinic to talk to his GP. But he's not been seen by the same GP twice in the last couple of years.'

He frowned. 'He told me his GP gave him the all-clear. Why would he lie to me about that?'

'I don't know,' she said. 'I guess he didn't think the scan was warranted. You know what young guys are like. They think they're bulletproof.'

Jake exhaled a breath in self-recrimination.

'I should've followed it up. I should have called the clinic myself.' He shoved his hand through his hair. 'What was so hard about telling me he didn't get it done, for God's sake?'

'You're his brother, Jake, not his doctor,' she said. 'Anyway, I thought I'd better scan him just to be on the safe side. He's got slightly irregular pupils.'

'He's probably stoned, that's why.'

'I don't think he's stoned or drunk.'

Jake curled his lip. 'Would you even recognise stoned and drunk if you saw it?'

Her grey eyes narrowed. 'What is that supposed to mean?'

'Maybe the circles you mix in do it with a little more class than my brother does,' he said. 'But I can tell you when someone is off his face and I don't need a bloody CT scan to confirm it. Every time I've seen Robbie lately he's been hungover.'

'You're letting your personal issues cloud your clinical judgement,' she said. 'That's why you should never treat your own family. You can miss things.'

'Let me tell you what I've *missed*, Dr Cargill,' Jake said through clenched teeth as fury and frustration threatened his ironclad control. 'I've *missed* having my kid brother around. In his place I've got some weird wacko who changes mood at the blink of an eye. I *miss* the way he used to come and talk to me about stuff. He looked up to me. I liked that I was his go-to person. It meant I was doing an all right job in my mother's place. I *miss* having a normal life, without spending hours worrying myself sick over what my brother's getting up, to or who else's brother or sister he's dragging into whatever sleazy little hellhole he chooses to live in. That's what I *miss*.'

The air rang with the echo of his harshly delivered words.

Her rounded grey eyes blinked at him a couple of times. 'It must be a nightmare for you,' she said.

Jake let out a ragged sigh and shoved his hand through his hair again. 'Sorry for shouting,' he said gruffly. 'None of this is your fault.'

'I'll let you know as soon as I get the results,' she said.

'Yeah,' he said with another weary sigh. 'You do that.'

# CHAPTER THIRTEEN

'ARE you sure?' Kitty asked the radiographer on duty a couple of hours later.

'Yes,' Peter Craven said. 'It's a meningioma.'

Kitty looked at the scans illuminated on the wall. 'How long do you think it's been there?' she asked.

'Quite some time, by the look of it.' He pointed to the wraparound features of the benign tumour. 'See how it's taken over the frontal lobe here and here?'

Kitty chewed at her lip. 'So that would account for some of the symptoms…'

'Personality change, moodiness, focal paralysis, hearing loss,' Peter said. He pushed back his chair. 'You'd better get Lewis Beck to have a look at it. He'd be the best neurosurgeon on staff to handle this sort of growth. Have you told Jake?'

'Not yet.'

'Want me to do it?'

Kitty shook her head. 'No, I'll tell him.'

Kitty found Jake in the A&E office writing up some patient notes. 'Jake?' she said. 'Can I have a word with you?'

He looked up from the notes, every muscle on his face slowly coming to a standstill as he read her grave expression. 'What's going on?' he asked.

'Robbie has a meningioma,' she said. 'It looks like he's had it a while—maybe several years.'

His dark blue eyes flickered with shock, his throat moving up and down as he swallowed. 'Are you sure?' he asked.

'Peter Craven just confirmed it,' she said.

The pen he'd been using fell out of his grasp and rolled across the desk. 'So…' he said. 'It wasn't a hangover.'

'No.'

He gave her an agonised look. 'I thought he was just being a rebellious kid. For all these months—the last two years—I've been at him to sort himself out, but it wasn't his fault.'

'Anyone would have assumed the same,' Kitty said. 'You weren't to know.'

He shook his head as if he couldn't quite believe it. 'If only I'd chased him up about that scan,' he said. 'Two years ago he started acting a bit weird. Do you think…?'

She nodded. 'Peter Craven thinks it must have only started causing symptoms fairly recently. It would have been easy to put them down to other things initially.'

'Have you told Robbie yet?' he asked.

'Not yet,' she said. 'I thought you might like to do it with me after you've seen the scans. He might cope better hearing it from you.'

He met her gaze with his hollowed one. 'You'd better show me the scans.'

Jake looked at the scans of his brother's brain and felt a tsunami of remorse and regret smash into him. Every word of criticism and correction came back to haunt him. Robbie had been sick for two years, maybe even longer. Even though he had done his best to rule out other causes, a part of him had too quickly assumed Robbie was running amok like so many of his peers.

How much precious time had been wasted? Why hadn't he physically taken him for the scan? He should have followed his brother through every step to make sure every base had been covered.

It was *his* fault Robbie had been sick for so long.

The truth stuck like a coat hanger in his throat.

He had done a lousy job of looking after his brother.

*He had failed.*

Kitty put a hand on his arm. 'It's not your fault, Jake,' she said, as if she had been reading his mind. 'His symptoms were mostly vague and intermittent up until now.'

'Of course it's my fault,' he said. 'How can it *not* be my fault?'

'It's always tricky diagnosing your own family,' she said. 'We can't even do a good job of diagnosing ourselves. We can't get the clinical objectivity.'

Jake pushed a hand through his hair. 'I should've picked this up.'

'How could you?' she asked. 'You're not his doctor.'

'I'm his brother, for God's sake,' he said. 'I should've seen the signs.'

'It's easy to see the signs in hindsight,' she said. 'But who's to know if some of his behaviour was simply like any other young guy kicking back against authority? You can't know for sure.'

He dragged a hand over his face. 'How am I going to make it up to him?'

'By being there for him now,' she said. 'That's all you can do. It's all he will want you to do.'

He expelled a long breath. 'I owe you an apology.'

'It's fine.'

'It's not fine,' he said. 'You're a damn good doctor, Kitty. I shouldn't have criticised you the way I did.'

'I still have a lot to learn,' she said. 'I think I do rely on testing too much. I don't have the confidence to trust my clinical judgement just yet.'

'It paid off this time,' he said. 'I dread to think how long Robbie would have gone on untreated if it hadn't been for you.'

'I'm sure you would have sorted it out eventually.'

Jake wasn't so sure about that. How long would it have taken him to see past his own prejudice? He didn't like to think of how long Robbie had suffered. And the fight wasn't even over—not by a long shot. The biggest battle lay ahead. Would his kid brother survive such complex surgery?

'Have you heard how Jake's brother's getting on?' Cathy asked at the end of the day in the locker room.

'He's got an appointment to see Lewis Beck tomorrow,' Kitty said. 'I guess he'll operate as soon as there's room on one of his lists.'

'How's Jake handling it?'

'It's been a terrible shock,' Kitty said. 'He blames himself.'

'Understandable, given the circumstances,' Cathy said.

Kitty chewed at her lip. 'I know, but it's not as if he could have done any different. Robbie admitted himself that he was struggling to cope. I automatically assumed he was depressed. If I hadn't noticed his other symptoms I might have sent him home with an appointment to see a counsellor, which he probably wouldn't have kept. He would have slipped through the cracks again.'

'Gwen was telling me how tough Jake has it with his family,' Cathy said.

'Yes…'

'Kind of makes you wonder if he's not quite as selfish and shallow as you first thought.'

'Yes,' Kitty said. 'There's certainly more to Jake Chandler than meets the eye.' She thought of how Robbie told her he'd been supposed to meet Jake last night but Robbie had decided against going at the last minute. Jake had probably spent hours looking for him out on the streets, as he had apparently done many times before.

'Well, I'm off home,' Cathy said. 'Do you need a lift? I can make a detour. It's not too far out of my way.'

'No, it's all right,' Kitty said. 'I want to check in on Robbie now he's been admitted to the ward. I'll make my way home after that.'

When Kitty got to Robbie's room Jake was sitting beside the bed looking even more haggard than he had earlier. He stood up as she came in.

'He's just drifted off to sleep,' he said. 'My sisters have been in to see him.'

'How is he?' she asked.

'A bit overwhelmed by it all,' he said, running a hand through his hair. 'We all are.'

'Is there anything I can do?' Kitty asked.

'No, we're fine,' he said. 'The girls would like to meet you some time. They want to thank you.'

'It was a lucky pick-up. I might have missed it on another day.'

'Don't be so humble,' he said. 'You taught me a valuable lesson. I've always prided myself on seeing the big picture. But I can see how attention to detail is just as important in some circumstances.'

'I guess it's all a matter of balance,' Kitty said. 'It would be foolish to waste time on a detailed history if a patient was bleeding internally.'

'Do you need a lift home?' he asked.

'I can catch a cab,' she said. 'I just wanted to make sure Robbie was settled in.'

'I'm heading off now, so I'll take you,' he said.

It was a mostly silent trip home. Kitty could tell Jake was still coming to terms with his brother's condition. She could only imagine how annoyed and frustrated he would be feeling with himself. Most men didn't like being in the wrong, but she suspected it would hit Jake harder than most. His family depended on him to look out for them. He had taken on that role from a young age. He had made sacrifices that she could only guess at in order to do the right thing by his family.

'Are you doing anything for dinner?' he suddenly asked.

Kitty glanced at him. 'Not really…'

'My place in an hour?'

She pulled at her lip with her teeth. 'I'm not sure…'

'Just dinner, OK?'

'Can I bring something?' she asked.

He gave her a smile that was worn about the edges. 'Just yourself.'

Kitty pulled yet another outfit out of her wardrobe. Everything was either too conservative or too casual. She had never felt so ill-prepared for a date. Not that it *was* a date.

It was just dinner.

*At his place.*

*Just the two of them.*

*Alone.*

Her stomach gave a nervous flutter. She didn't trust herself alone with Jake Chandler. He was too attractive, too masculine, and way too tempting. Her self-control completely disappeared when he touched her. Even worse was that she *wanted* him to touch her. She wanted him to make her forget about her principles and her neat and orderly plans for the future. She wanted him to make her feel something other than the luke-warm emotions she had settled for in the past. He made her feel vibrantly alive in every cell of her being. He made her heart race and her pulse pound. He made her body ache with longing— an intense ache she could feel every time he so much as looked at her with those dark blue eyes of his. Those eyes saw what she tried so hard to hide. He saw the need she shied away from. He saw the hunger. He saw how he made her feel.

* * *

Kitty took a steadying breath and tapped on his door. She heard Jake's firm tread and then the door opened. Her heart tripped and her breath caught somewhere in the middle of her chest. He had shaved, but his hair was still damp from his shower and it looked as if he had recently combed it with his fingers. He was wearing jeans and a black cotton casual shirt; the sleeves were rolled up halfway along his forearms, revealing his strong wrists. She smelt of the sharp citrus scent of sun-warmed lemons.

'Hi…' she said, thrusting a bottle of wine at his mid-section. 'I'm not sure if it's any good. I'm not really an expert or anything.'

'I'm sure it'll be fine,' he said. 'Come in.'

'I hope you haven't gone to too much trouble,' she said.

'No trouble at all,' he said, closing the door. 'You look nice. You smell nice too.'

Kitty wished she didn't blush so easily. She was so damned transparent. No wonder his eyes were always glinting at her. 'How long have you lived here?' she asked to fill in the silence.

'Four years,' he said, leading the way to the kitchen. 'I've thought about moving a few times but haven't got around to it yet.'

'Because of Robbie?'

He glanced at her before he reached for two wine glasses. 'Not just Robbie,' he said. 'My sisters have needed a bit of support over the years. I've put a lot of stuff on hold. But I figure they would've done the same in my place.'

'You've been a wonderful brother, Jake.'

He made a self-deprecating sound as he poured the wine. 'Yeah, haven't I just?'

'I mean it,' she said. 'You have to stop blaming yourself about Robbie's condition. You know the stats. People can have a meningioma for decades without symptoms.'

He passed her a glass of wine. 'I should've ruled out everything else first before I started criticising him,' he said. 'I should've insisted on seeing the scans for myself. How could I have been so easily fobbed off? I'll tell you why,' he said, before she could answer. 'I *wanted* to believe he was acting irresponsibly. Why? Because I *resented* his freedom to do so. Here was I, giving up years of my life to make sure he and the girls got the best chance in life, and I *resented* that he didn't have to make a single sacrifice.'

Kitty reached out and touched him on the arm. 'I know how you must feel.'

'How can you possibly know?' he asked with an embittered expression. 'You're an only child. You've never had to watch out for anyone but yourself. How can you *possibly* know?'

Kitty shifted her gaze from his hardened one. She put her glass down and slipped off the stool she had perched on. 'Maybe I should leave you to wallow in your guilt,' she said. 'It's obvious I'm not much help to you.'

He stopped her at the door with a hand on her wrist. 'No,' he said, blowing out a long breath. 'Don't go. I'm sorry. Forgive me?'

She looked into his eyes and felt her heart give a stumble. 'This is a difficult time for you...I don't want to make things worse.'

'You're not making worse,' he said, absently stroking her wrist with his thumb. 'I want you here. I wouldn't have asked you if I didn't.'

Kitty felt herself drowning in the deep blue

sea of his eyes. Her skin was tingling where he was stroking it. Her desire for him was unfurling inside her like the petals of an exotic flower. Her pulse quickened and her breath caught as his eyes slipped to her mouth. 'I'm not used to doing this...' she said.

'It's just dinner, Kitty.'

She moistened her lips. 'Is it?'

His eyes locked on hers. 'Do you want it to be something else?'

'I'm not sure...'

He brushed her cheek with an idle finger. 'I'm not going to deny that I want to make love to you,' he said. 'But whether I do or not is entirely up to you.'

Kitty looked at his mouth again. Was it possible to want a man so much you didn't care about anything else but the physical sensation of being in his arms? What did emotions have to do with it anyway? It was a physical need. Their bodies were designed for pleasure. The chemistry she felt with him was surely enough for now.

'The work thing...' she said, frowning. 'I hate the thought of everyone talking.'

'We can keep this out of the corridors and locker rooms,' he said. 'This is between us. It's no one else's business.'

She looked into his eyes. 'I don't want to be a one-night stand.'

'You won't be.'

'I don't want to fall in love with you, either.'

'Wise girl.'

'I mean it, Jake,' she said, putting her hands on his chest. 'I want to keep things uncomplicated.'

'No promises,' he said as he drew her closer. 'No strings.'

Kitty felt his body thicken against her. It was all she could do to stop from tearing his clothes from his body. She wanted to explore him with her hands and mouth. Ever since she had seen him naked this morning she had secretly fantasised about touching him, stroking him, holding him.

'I want you,' she said, in a voice she barely recognised as her own: it was husky, breathy, womanly.

'There's something I have to do first,' he said.

'What's that?'

'This,' he said, reaching behind her head to release the clasp that confined her hair so it tumbled freely around her shoulders.

And then his head came down slowly, ever so slowly, until his mouth stole her breath away in a kiss that branded her finally as his.

# CHAPTER FOURTEEN

KITTY felt the red-hot urgency that coursed through him as his mouth ravaged hers. It whipped along her nerve-endings like an electric current, making her vibrate with longing within seconds. She clawed at him with wild hands, desperate to feel his skin against hers, to taste the salt of his flesh, to explore the contours of his body, to have him at her mercy.

She got under his shirt and stroked his chest with her hands, but it wasn't enough.

She wanted to feel *him*.

She worked at his trouser fastening, finally releasing it to claim her prize. He was powerfully aroused, hard and thick, swollen with the need she could feel hammering through his blood.

His mouth ground against hers, hungry and insatiable. Her skin shivered all over in delight as he roughly tugged at her clothes. His mouth captured her breast, sucking on it, releasing it to stroke it with his tongue, and then sucking on it again. He did the same to her other breast, making her cry out loud with the spine-tingling pleasure of it.

He went back to her mouth, walking her backwards out of the room. A stool fell over, a picture on the wall got dislodged, a lamp on a table in the hallway almost fell to the floor, but still he didn't lift his mouth off hers.

Kitty felt a mattress underneath her back and then his body coming down over her. She clung to him, kissing him back with heated fervour as he was kissing her.

Somehow she wriggled out of her clothes, while he dispensed with his in between passionate kisses and caresses that made her gasp and cry out loud.

'Now,' she panted as he came back over her, pinning her with his weight.

'Not yet,' he said, moving down her body with his hot mouth. 'I have things to do.'

Kitty snatched in a breath as he kissed and stroked his way down to her belly button. She dug her fingers into his hair as he went lower. This was new territory for her. She didn't know if she could do this. It was too intimate.

'Relax,' he said. 'You're too tense.'

'I can't.'

'Yes, you can,' he said. 'Let your thighs go. That's it. Trust me. I won't rush you. Take all the time you need.'

She closed her eyes and let herself go with the sensations as he explored her with soft strokes of his tongue. The tension built and built. All her nerves seemed to be gathered at one point, hovering there for some final trigger to catapult her over the edge.

At last she was there.

She soared over the precipice, free falling into a whirling sea of powerful sensations that drove every thought out of her head. She was suspended, floating, drifting in a world she hadn't visited before, an erotic world of delights and delicious feelings of satiation.

'Oh, God...' She put a hand over her eyes, suddenly shy at how undone she had become.

Jake came back over her, tugging her hand

away from her face. 'Hey,' he said. 'Don't hide from me.'

'I can't believe you just did that,' she said. 'I can't believe *I* just did that.'

'You haven't done that before?'

'I've never felt comfortable about it,' she confessed.

He brushed her hair back off her face. 'Every couple has their comfort zones,' he said. 'What's right for one will not always be right for another.'

'I can imagine there's not much you haven't been comfortable with,' Kitty said.

He gave a could-mean-anything smile. 'I have my boundaries.'

She ran her hands over his chest, slowly tiptoeing her fingers below his navel. 'I guess I'll have to figure out what they are, won't I?'

'I can hardly wait,' he said, and covered her mouth with his.

Kitty hadn't thought it possible to feel the same level of desire so soon, but within moments she was writhing beneath him, aching for the completion she craved. She felt him hard against her, close but not close enough. She caressed him, delighting in the way he responded with a deep groan as she moved over the blunt tip of him. She felt the ooze of his pre-ejaculating fluid—that primal response of his body that left her in no doubt of how much he wanted her.

He reached past her for a condom in one of the bedside drawers. She pushed aside the thought of all the other women he had done this with before. She had gone into this with her eyes wide open. She had known she wasn't the first. She knew she wouldn't be the last.

'What's wrong?' he asked.

Kitty painted on a carefree smile. 'Nothing.'

He captured her chin, his eyes holding hers. 'We don't have to do this if you're not ready,' he said.

'I am ready,' she said. 'It's just I can't help thinking of how many times you've done this. Do you say and do the same thing each and every time?'

He frowned. 'This is about us, Kitty. It's not about anyone else. What we experience together is unique.'

'If you close your eyes I could be just anyone.'

'You're not just anyone,' he said. 'You're you. You taste different. You feel different. You smell different. You *are* different.'

She circled one of his flat nipples with her finger. 'I want you to always remember this,' she said. 'You know…long after I've gone back to England.' She looked into his eyes. 'Will you promise me that?'

He took her hand and kissed her fingertips. 'I thought we agreed on no promises.'

'Just this one.'

He held her gaze for a heartbeat. 'I promise.'

She traced his top lip with her fingertip. 'You're a lot nicer on closer inspection, Jake Chandler,' she said. 'I think I might not detest you quite so much after all.'

He gave her a cautionary look. 'You're not falling in love with me, are you?'

'Not a chance,' she said, and pulled his head down until his mouth met hers.

Jake lay awake in the early hours of the morning, not sure what was wrong until he realised Kitty was still lying in the bed beside him. He had a rule he stuck to rigorously. No sleepovers. It made the boundaries blur too much. He didn't care for the morning-after routine. Women had a tendency to see things differently in the cold hard light of morning. In spite of everything they said to the contrary they *always* wanted more than he was prepared to give. Before he knew it there would be a toothbrush left in his bathroom or a few items of clothes left in his wardrobe.

It was simpler to avoid the issue.

No one got hurt that way.

Last night he had acted on primal instincts alone. He had wanted to connect with Kitty physically, to feel the movement of her body around him, to remind himself of the rhythms of life. He had wanted to block out the mental anguish of his guilt. But those few precious moments of oblivion had done much more than release him from his torment. His body had recognised something in her that spoke to him much more than just physically. It had been like hearing a language he'd thought he had forgotten. The caress of her mouth and hands hadn't felt like just another sexual partner delivering pleasure. Her hands and mouth had felt worshipful, reverent almost. Her tentative touch and her passionate responses had awoken in him a desire to feel more than sexual satisfaction.

He looked at her in the silvery light of the moon. She was lying on her side, the cotton sheet draped over her slim form, showing every delightful contour from her neat bottom and thighs to her creamy breasts. Her hair was like a fluffy cloud around her head. He couldn't help reaching out and running his fingers through it, tethering himself to her via those silky strands. She gave a little murmur and nestled closer into the pillow, her lips curved in a small but blissful smile.

He leaned down and pressed a soft kiss to the satiny skin of her shoulder. She smelt of fresh flowers, but he also picked up a faint trace of his own masculine scent clinging to her skin that made something shift deep inside his stomach, like a gear slipping from its cogs.

She opened her eyes and smiled at him shyly. 'What time is it?'

Jake brushed a strand of hair off her forehead

while he mentally shoved that gear back into line. 'Time you were tucked up in your own bed,' he said.

A flicker of hurt passed through her gaze. 'You want me to leave?' she asked.

'We both have to work in the morning,' he said, getting up from the bed and reaching for his boxer shorts and stepping into them. He went over to the window and stared sightlessly at the view. 'It's going to be a big day for Robbie. I want to be there for him.'

Jake heard the soft padding of her footsteps over the carpet, and then he felt her arms gently encircle his waist from behind. He put one of his hands over her linked ones, his body already aching to have her again. He felt her cheek rest against his back, her soft breath like a caress over his skin.

After a few moments he turned around and cradled her face in his hands, his eyes holding hers. 'You really should go home while you've got the chance,' he said.

She held his look with those soft grey eyes of

hers. 'Maybe I'm not ready to be sent off home like a child who's overstayed her welcome.'

He stroked the cushion of her bottom lip with one of his thumbs. 'Maybe I don't want company right now,' he said, while his body betrayed him shamelessly where it was surging against the softness of hers.

She gave him a coy smile. 'Maybe you're lying.'

He brought his mouth down just above hers. 'Maybe you're right,' he said, and covered her lips with his.

Kitty slipped out of Jake's bed while he was still sleeping, just as dawn was breaking. She carried her shoes and was almost at the front door when he came out of the bedroom with just a towel draped around his hips.

'You should've woken me,' he said, rubbing a hand over his stubbly jaw.

'I wasn't sure what the protocol was,' Kitty said, dropping her shoes to place her feet in them.

He frowned and let his hand fall by his side. 'Are you angry with me?'

She shrugged. 'Why would I be angry? You told me the rules. No strings. No promises.'

There was a taut little silence.

'I liked having you stay last night,' he said. 'I liked it a lot.'

Kitty searched his gaze for a moment. 'I liked it too.'

He came over to where she was standing. Her body was within a mere hair's breadth of his. She could feel the sensual energy transmitting from his body to hers. Her insides seemed to shift inside her in an effort to bridge that tiny distance.

'I'd like to see you after work,' he said. 'Let's have dinner. I'll book somewhere on the water-front in Rushcutters Bay.'

Kitty was conscious of the emotionally charged day ahead for him. 'What if I cook dinner for you at my place?' she suggested.

He gave her a ghost of a smile. 'The way to a man's heart?'

'I think it would take a lot more than my meagre culinary ability to break through *that* stronghold,' she said lightly.

His eyes studied hers for a heartbeat or two. 'I've never spent the whole night with anyone before,' he said.

Kitty raised her brows. 'One of your rules?'

'Sort of,' he said. 'I don't usually sleep well with someone else in the room, let alone the bed.'

'I hope I didn't snore.'

His mouth tilted in another smile. 'No, you were very quiet,' he said. 'I hardly knew you were there.'

'Such scintillating company,' Kitty said. 'I'll have to lift my game.'

His gaze waltzed with hers in a sensual two-step, each step incrementally tightening the tension that simmered between them. 'Have you got time for breakfast?' he asked.

'I've sort of got in the habit of skipping it.'

'It's the most important meal of the day.'

'So I've heard.'

He circled her waist with his arms and brought

her flush against his body. 'You don't know what you're missing,' he said.

A tremor shuddered through her body. 'As of last night, I think I do,' she said. 'But I really need to shower and get ready for work. I have this boss who might fire me if I turn up late.'

'I'm sure if you just smiled at him he'd melt.'

Kitty smiled at him and watched as his dark blue eyes softened. 'Great tip—thanks,' she said. 'I'll keep it in mind.'

He pressed a brush-like kiss to her mouth. 'I'll meet you in the car park in half an hour,' he said. 'I'll drive you to my mate the mechanic's to pick up your car.'

'I can catch a cab,' Kitty said.

He trailed a finger down her cheek. 'Half an hour,' he said. 'Don't be late.'

It was close to lunchtime before Kitty saw Jake on the unit. He was walking past just as she was coming out of Bay Three, where she had finished assessing an elderly patient with a broken wrist. She almost ran into him, but he steadied her with his hands.

'Sorry,' he said. 'I wasn't looking where I was going.'

Kitty looked at the shadow of worry in his eyes. 'Is everything all right?' she asked.

He dropped his hands from her arms. 'Lewis Beck wants to operate today,' he said. 'He shuffled his cases around to fit Robbie in this afternoon. It's all happening so fast. This time yesterday I thought my brother was just a layabout jerk. Now I'm facing the prospect of losing him.'

Kitty touched him on the arm. 'Robbie's in very good hands, Jake,' she said.

'I can't tell you how many times I've tried to allay patients and their relatives' fears over surgical procedures,' he said. 'But it's so different when it's your own relative. Robbie's my kid brother. He's only twenty-four. He's got his whole life ahead of him. What if something goes wrong?'

'Nothing will go wrong, Jake,' Kitty said. 'He's young and otherwise healthy. You have to stay positive for his sake as well as your own.'

He scraped a hand through his hair. 'I know, I

know.' He dropped his hand and gave her a brief thin-lipped smile. 'Thanks.'

'No problem.'

He glanced at his watch. 'I'd better get back to see Robbie before they take him down to Theatre,' he said. 'Any problems here?'

'No, everything's fine,' Kitty said. 'Lei's a great registrar. We've got things covered.'

'Good,' he said. 'I'll be back as soon as I can.'

Jake waited until the anaesthetist had done his pre-surgical assessment before he entered Robbie's room. 'How are you feeling?' he asked.

'Nervous,' Robbie said. 'I'm not sure I like the thought of my head being cut open.'

'The scar will be a great talking point,' Jake said.

'I'll look like a skinhead until my hair grows back.'

'Robbie,' Jake began, 'there's something I need to say—'

'It's cool, Jake,' Robbie said. 'I was a jerk not to get the scan done. Jen and Rosie chewed my ears off about it earlier this morning. They said it's made it so much harder on you. That you feel guilty. That you feel it's your fault or something. But it's not. I'm an adult. I should've got myself checked out.'

Jake grasped his brother's hand. 'I'm sorry for not being there for you. I can't believe how badly I handled things.'

'You've managed things just fine,' Robbie said. 'You always do. You're there for all of us, all the time. I've been thinking about it…you know, while I've been lying here doing nothing. You stepped up to the plate when Mum died. No one asked you if you wanted to. You just did it.'

'I wanted to do it.'

'Yeah, but it's not been easy, has it?' Robbie said. 'You've made a lot of sacrifices for us. When Rosie got pregnant, for instance. You were really looking forward to that trip. I know you were. If things had been different you could've worked overseas for a couple of years. But you didn't get the chance. You gave it up for us.'

Jake shrugged it off. 'I'll head overseas some time.'

'That English doctor seems nice,' Robbie said. 'What's the story with you two?'

Jake smiled. 'She's a sweetheart, isn't she?'

Robbie's brows lifted. 'Does Rosie know about this?'

'You know about that stupid bet, huh?'

'Rosie told me,' Robbie said, and punched him playfully on the upper arm. 'Looks like you'd better pay up.'

'It is that obvious?' Jake asked.

Robbie gave his eyes a little roll. 'You were always going to lose, Jake.'

'Yeah, well, I was going great guns until Kitty Cargill came along,' Jake said.

Robbie grinned. 'That's what I meant.'

# CHAPTER FIFTEEN

BEFORE Kitty left work she spoke to Jake, who informed her Robbie's surgery had gone well and that he was now in recovery. Jake planned to wait until he was moved to the high dependency unit before he came home to have dinner with her.

Kitty was making a mango, rocket and feta cheese salad when her mobile started to ring. She picked it up without checking the caller ID. 'Hello?'

'Kitty, it's me—Sophie... Please don't hang up.'

Kitty drew in a little breath. 'I'm kind of busy right now,' she said. 'I have someone coming for dinner in a few minutes.'

'I won't hold you up...it's just that I really miss you,' Sophie said. 'I never thought it would be like this... You know, you so far away when I'm about to get married.'

*Well, if you hadn't pinched my future husband maybe I'd be there right by your side as your maid of honour, as we'd always planned since we were seven years old*, she thought.

'Sophie, this isn't a good time,' she said.

'I'm sorry,' Sophie said with a sob in her voice. 'I didn't want to hurt you like this. Charles and I fought it for so long.'

'How long?' Kitty asked.

'Remember that trip we all took to the Cotswolds a couple of years ago?'

'Yes,' Kitty said, seething with resentment as she thought of how she had got held up at the hospital and Charles had gone ahead with Sophie. She had come down later with their other friends, Tom and Claire and Finn. 'How convenient it must have been for you both to spend the first night down there without anyone else to interrupt your little love tryst.'

'It wasn't like that, Kitty,' Sophie said. 'We didn't do anything. We just talked. I was going out with Finn, as you know, but things weren't really working out. Charles was so supportive. He told me I shouldn't be wasting Finn's time if I wasn't truly in love with him.'

'What a pity he didn't take his own advice,' Kitty put in.

Sophie sighed. 'He loved you, Kitty. He still loves you. But not the way a man should love the woman he's going to marry and spend the rest of his life with.'

'He could have told me rather than have me find out the way I did,' Kitty said.

'I'm so sorry about that,' Sophie said. 'It just happened. You have to believe that. Our feelings got the better of us. We'd planned to tell you that night. It was a horrible way for you to find out. I was so ashamed. I couldn't believe I'd lost control like that. It started with a kiss and then suddenly we were in bed and… Well, you know the rest.'

Kitty pressed her lips together, her thoughts going to the kiss that had been her sensual undoing with Jake. Did she have the right to judge Sophie when she had been guilty of the very same loss of control?

Of course she had the right.

It was *totally* different.

Neither she nor Jake had betrayed anyone else in indulging their passion for each other. It was all very well for Sophie to apologise, but it didn't change the fact that her two best friends in the whole world had betrayed her in the most despicable, hurtful way.

'Look, Sophie, I really have to go,' she said. 'I appreciate the phone call, but I think it's best if we all get on with our lives and leave it at that.'

'Remember when we were little girls?' Sophie said. 'Remember when we promised each other we'd be each other's maid of honour?'

'We're not little girls any more,' Kitty said. 'Now, if you don't mind, I—'

'I won't feel married if you're not there,' Sophie said. 'It won't be the same without you. We'll be one down on the wedding party. I'm not going to ask anyone to take your place. The photos are going to look rubbish.'

'I'm sure Claire or Harriet will do a perfectly fine job of being your bridesmaid and maid of honour,' Kitty said.

'I don't want Claire or Harriet,' Sophie said. 'I want *you*. We promised, remember?'

Kitty looked at the promise ring that was creating a ridge in the flesh of her finger. 'Not all promises can be kept,' she said, and ended the call.

Jake knocked on Kitty's door and listened as her footsteps approached. The door opened and he smiled at her. 'Sorry I'm late,' he said, handing her a bottle of champagne.

'How's Robbie?' she asked.

'Awake and flirting with the nurses in HDU,' he said. 'The operation went well. Lewis Beck is confident he'll be out of hospital within a week.'

'I'm so glad,' Kitty said. 'You must be feeling very relieved.'

'Yeah,' Jake said, following her to the kitchen. 'Hey, what's cooking? It smells delicious.'

'Nothing fancy,' she said.

'No cucumber sandwiches?'

She gave him a half-hearted smile before she went in search of glasses. 'No.'

'Here, let me get those for you,' he said as she tried to reach the cupboard above her head.

'I don't think there are any champagne glasses in there,' she said.

'Nothing wrong with drinking champagne out of a wine glass,' Jake said. 'Especially tonight, when we're celebrating.'

She gave him another slightly distracted smile as she tucked a little strand of hair behind her ear. 'Of course.'

Jake put the glasses on the bench beside the champagne and put his hands about her waist, bringing her a little closer. 'What's up?' he asked.

She looked at his shirtfront. 'Nothing.'

'Hey, remember that I've got two sisters,' Jake said. 'I know enough about women to know that "nothing" means "something", and it's usually something big. So spill it. Tell me what's worrying you.'

She slowly raised her grey eyes to his. 'My ex-best friend called a few minutes ago,' she said.

'The one who hooked up with your ex?'

A resentful glitter sparked in her eyes. 'She wants me to be her maid of honour at their wedding,' she said. 'Can you believe that? As if I'd stand at the altar and smile for the cameras while she promises to love the man I thought I was going to marry! Everyone would be staring at me, pitying me—or, worse, laughing at me.'

Jake frowned in empathy. 'I can understand how tough a gig it would be for you, but wouldn't it be better to tough it out? Show them you're over it? No one will laugh at you. They'll be pleased you've moved on with your life.'

She chewed at her lip for a moment. 'I'm not ready to pretend everything's OK,' she said. 'Why should I let them have a perfect day when they've ruined everything for me?'

'Aren't you being a little bit selfish about this?' he asked.

Her frown was quick and deep. 'Selfish?' she said. 'What do you mean?'

'It's selfish to want them to suffer for your misery,' he said. 'You need to let it go, Kitty. You being angry and resentful won't stop them loving each other. Charles has made his choice. So it wasn't you? Move on. Be the bigger person. Show them how mature and grown-up you are about it all.'

Her frown relaxed a little but her mouth was still pushed forward in a little pout. 'They're the ones who are being selfish,' she said. 'They've wrecked my life.'

'Have they?' Jake asked, pulling her closer. 'Have they really?'

Her eyes meshed with his.

Jake brushed his thumb over her bottom lip. 'We wouldn't be together now if it hadn't been for them,' he said. 'You wouldn't have come all this way and turned my world upside down, not to mention make me lose a cool one thousand bucks.'

Her mouth twitched with a ghost of a smile. 'Was it worth it?' she asked.

Jake put a hand in the curve of her back to draw her even closer as he lowered his mouth to hers. 'Best thousand bucks I've ever spent,' he said, and kissed her.

Kitty leaned into Jake's kiss, her body responding to the hot hard heat of him surging against her in arrant maleness. She felt her stomach flip in excitement as his tongue boldly commanded entry to her mouth. She opened to him, whimpering in delight. Her breasts started to ache with the need to feel his touch. She rubbed against him with wanton abandon, her lower body pulsing with the need to feel his possession. She felt the honeyed slickness between her thighs.

He slipped her top off one of her shoulders and worked his way with his mouth over her sensitive skin, over her collarbone, against her neck, to just below her ear. She felt her flesh rise in tiny goosebumps as his teeth tugged at her earlobe. She rose on tiptoe to subject him to the same sensual assault. She delighted in the deep groan he gave when she tugged his shirt out of his trousers. She ran her hands over his chest, over his pectoral muscles and the taut ridges of his toned abdomen. She boldly unfastened his trousers and sought him with her hand. He groaned again as she stroked him. He was so hard and heavy she could feel the throb of his blood against her fingers.

Her insides clamped with lust. It was a consuming force that would allow no other outcome but satiation. She trailed her mouth down over his chest, down, down, down, breathing in the pure male scent of him, teasing him with her teeth and her tongue.

He put his hands on her shoulders to halt her, but she continued determinedly on her erotic journey of discovery. She wanted to pleasure him, to have him at the mercy of his need for her. She wanted to prove how exciting she could be as a lover—not just to him, but also to herself. She wanted to taste him. To feel him shudder with release.

He fisted a hand in her hair, groaning again as she took him in her mouth after he'd quickly put on a condom. She felt him brace himself; his thighs rock-hard and slightly apart. She continued on her mission, relishing his response. She felt the exact moment he climaxed. It was so intensely intimate to receive him in such a way.

'Oh, God,' he said shakily. 'This is the most amazing dinner party I've ever been to.'

Kitty smiled as she straightened. 'That's just

for starters,' she said. 'Just wait until you see what I've got for dessert.'

His eyes glinted as he backed her against the kitchen bench. 'That must mean that the main course is up to me,' he said.

Kitty shivered when his hands pulled her top over her head. He tossed it to the floor at their feet and then went to her skirt. He slid the zip down at the back and stroked his hands over her bottom. Her bra and knickers soon joined her skirt and top. She was standing there stark naked, but for some reason she didn't feel embarrassed. Instead she felt powerfully feminine. The way his gaze devoured her made her skin tingle and her spine melt. She could see the passionate intention in those dark blue depths and it made every hair on her head tingle at the roots.

He spun her around so her back was to him. Her breath hitched in her throat as she felt him nudging between her quivering thighs. She clutched at the counter-top to steady herself, every nerve screaming for his first thrust. She gasped when he surged into her, her body accepting him with slick moist heat. He drove to the hilt; his movements slow at first, but then gradually building to a pace that carried her at breathtaking speed to the summit of human pleasure.

She sobbed as her body shuddered and shook with aftershocks, the spasms of her body triggering his final plunge into paradise. She felt him move against her as he emptied himself; his groans of ecstasy making her feel more like a woman than she had ever felt before.

Jake turned her around to face him. 'You're amazing,' he said, stroking his hands up and down her upper arms.

Kitty tried to play it cool and casual and looked at him from beneath her lowered lashes in a coquettish manner. 'I bet you say that to all the girls.'

A small frown pulled at his brow. 'Actually, I don't,' he said. 'There's sex and there's sex— or so I've always thought. But sex with you is something completely different.'

Kitty wanted to believe him. It had certainly felt that way to her. What she had experienced with him was so far from her experience with her ex that it was as if she were in a different body.

But she knew the rules of being involved with Jake.

This was not for the long term. She would be going back to Britain before too long. He would continue with his playboy no-strings lifestyle.

*They would probably never see or hear from each other again.*

She pushed aside the ache that thought caused and gave him a bright smile. 'Why don't you open the champagne while I get dressed?'

His eyes ran over her like a hot blue-tipped flame. 'I've got an even better idea,' he said. 'Why don't you stay just the way you are?'

'I can't eat dinner with no clothes on,' she said, giving him a shocked look. 'What on earth would the neighbours think?'

He gave her a wolfish smile as he reached for her. 'I can't speak for the others, but personally I have no problem with it.'

Kitty shivered in delight as he bent his head

to her neck. 'What about dinner?' she asked. 'Aren't you hungry yet?'

'Starving,' he said as he swooped down and captured her mouth.

# CHAPTER SIXTEEN

'TODAY'S the big day,' Kitty said to Robbie when she visited him on her tea break a few days later. 'I hear you're going home.'

'Yeah,' Robbie said. 'I can't wait to get out of here.'

'Has it been that bad?'

'Not really, but I'm sick of being a patient,' he said. 'Jake and the girls keep fussing over me like I'm going to have some sort of relapse.'

'That's because they love you,' Kitty said. 'You're lucky you have siblings who are always looking out for you.'

'I know, but I want to get on with my life,' he said. 'I want to re-enrol at university. If I get my skates on I won't be too far behind.'

'Are you sure you're not rushing things?' Kitty asked. 'You've been through a big operation. You still need time to heal. It's only been a week.

A three-hour anaesthetic knocks most people around a bit.'

'I'll be fine,' he said. 'I feel great. I know I look like something from a horror movie, but I feel good.'

Kitty smiled. 'Are you going to stay with Jake for a few days? He said he'd offered to look after you.'

Robbie gave a shrug. 'For a day or two maybe… I kind of figure Jake needs his own space. I can always stay with Jen or Rosie after that.'

'I'm sure he would be happy to look after you,' Kitty said. 'He's already planned to take a few days off. We talked about it last night.'

Robbie looked at her. 'You're good for him, Kitty,' he said. 'He's happier than I've ever seen him before.'

'I'm sure that has much more to do with you getting better than anything to do with me,' she said.

Robbie frowned. 'You love him, though, don't you?'

Kitty was momentarily caught off guard. She

tried not to think about her feelings for Jake. She pushed those thoughts aside every time they surfaced. She had spent a lot of time with him over the last few days. The hospital network was buzzing about their affair, but she had weathered it much better than she had expected. She had even met his sisters on a couple of occasions and had felt totally at ease. It was hard not to, given that the girls and Robbie were so lovely and friendly. Just like the siblings she'd always wished she'd had.

She hadn't wanted to admit to herself how much she enjoyed being with Jake. She had accepted the affair for what it was: a brief interlude that was part of her master plan to put her heartbreak over Charles and Sophie behind her. But somehow as each day passed she found it harder and harder to recall Charles's features, let alone his kisses.

*All she could think of was Jake.*

Her body felt him for hours after they'd made love. It was like carrying a part of him with her wherever she went.

She didn't want it to end.

She didn't want *them* to end.

'I'm heading back to Britain for Easter,' she said, adopting a carefree tone. 'I've really enjoyed being here, though. I've learned heaps.'

Robbie looked at her with studied concentration. 'Maybe Jake will come and visit you over there some time,' he said. 'He's always wanted to travel. He pretends he doesn't but really he does. He's given up everything for the girls and me. I wish he'd just live his own life for a change. He deserves to be happy.'

'I guess he's been taking care of you all for so long he doesn't know any other way to be happy,' she said. 'You'll have to show him you're perfectly capable of looking after yourselves.' She gave his hand a little squeeze. 'I'd better get going. A&E is probably stacked to the ceiling with patients by now.'

Robbie lifted his fingers off the bed in a farewell wave. 'See you around.'

Jake came home from work ten days later to see Robbie had packed his things and placed them by the front door. 'What's going on?' he said.

'It's time I got my own place,' Robbie said. 'I'm crowding you.'

'You're not crowding me,' Jake said, tossing his jacket over the back of the sofa. 'We've talked about this already. You can stay as long as you want. There's plenty of room.'

'But what about you and Kitty?' Robbie asked. 'You've only been over to her place a couple of times, and when she comes over here I can tell she feels she's in the way.'

'Kitty understands how things are right now,' Jake said. 'My priority is to get you back on your feet.'

'But it's not fair to her or to you,' Robbie said. 'She'll be going back before you know it, and you've hardly had any time together.'

Jake hated being reminded of Kitty's return to Britain. It was like a nagging toothache that he could mostly ignore if no one brought his attention to it. But even the staff at the hospital had taken it upon themselves to remind him of it lately. He had tried to play down his involvement with her, and Kitty too had been very tight-lipped, but it was hard to pretend he didn't enjoy having her in his life both at work and in private. Those precious few private moments he'd snatched with her over the last couple of weeks had taken on a special meaning.

'What's brought this on?' he asked.

Robbie shrugged. 'I just thought it was time to get out of your hair.'

'But I don't understand,' Jake said, frowning. 'What's the point of paying rent you can ill afford right now? It doesn't make sense when there's a room going begging here.'

'Kitty thinks it's best if I start to take more responsibility for myself,' Robbie said. 'And the girls too. We all rely on you too much. It's time we stood on our own feet.'

Jake felt his spine stiffen and his brows snapped together. 'Did *she* suggest you move out?' he asked.

'Not in so many words…'

'How many words?' Jake growled. 'For God's sake, Robbie, you've just had major surgery. You can't go back to living a normal life as if nothing's happened. Kitty shouldn't have put such a damn-fool crazy idea in your head. She has no right to get involved in what's none of her damn business.'

Robbie looked worried. 'You're not going to get mad at her, are you?' he asked.

'Get mad?' Jake asked clenching his jaw. 'I *am* mad. I'm furious with her.'

'You can't stop me from moving out,' Robbie said. 'Anyway, I think she's right. You take on too much, Jake. You've been a substitute parent for so long you don't know how to be a brother any more.'

Jake felt a strange ache in the middle of his chest. How long since he *had* been simply a brother? It seemed like decades.

*It was decades.*

'Where are you going to stay?' he asked, glancing at Robbie's bag.

'A mate of mine's got a place in Glebe,' Robbie said. 'It'll be close to uni. I'll be able to walk since I'm not allowed to drive just yet.'

'I'm not happy about this,' Jake said with a concerned frown, his gut churning with the pain of letting go. Was this some sort of crazy empty nest syndrome he was feeling? How was he supposed to stop worrying? How could he trust that Robbie would be all right? 'It's still early days. You shouldn't be taking any risks at this stage.'

'I'm fine, Jake,' Robbie said, reaching for his bag. 'I want to get my life back. You need to get yours back as well.'

'My life is fine just the way it is,' Jake said. *Or at least it was until a little English rose came along and poked her uptilted nose where it doesn't belong.*

Robbie put out his hand. 'Thanks for everything.'

Jake pushed Robbie's hand out of the way and gathered him in a big brother hug. 'Take care of yourself, Robbie,' he said gruffly.

Kitty had not long got back from orchestra rehearsal when she saw Jake stalking across the courtyard to her town house. She had tried to give him as much space as he and Robbie needed, but it had been so hard to keep away. Each time he looked at her she felt a thousand delicious sensations wash over her. At work they had been nothing but professional, but still when he locked gazes with her she felt the electric current of their connection pass through her entire body.

She opened the door before he pressed the doorbell. 'I was going to call you,' she said, smiling brightly. 'I made some pancakes earlier. I thought you and Robbie might like some for supper.'

His expression was as dark as thunder. 'Robbie's gone.'

'Gone?'

'Don't play the innocent with me,' he said, frowning at her savagely. 'You know damn well he's packed up and left. You were the one who bloody suggested it.'

Kitty felt a little rattle of unease move down her spine. She had never seen Jake so angry. She could feel the menacing waves of it crackling through the air towards her. She refused to be intimidated, however.

'Robbie is an adult,' she said. 'You can't keep him and your sisters chained to your side in case something goes wrong in their lives. You can't always be there to pick up the pieces. How are they ever going to learn to take care of themselves if all they ever have to do is call you and you fix things for them?'

His frown was a deep V between his brows. 'What the hell would *you* know about what it takes to be a family?' he asked. 'You with your crackpot parents who haven't even got the guts to commit to each other full-time.'

Kitty lifted one of her brows. 'Isn't that a little bit rich, coming from you?'

'What do you mean by that?'

She rolled her eyes in disdain. 'Jake, you're the biggest commitment-phobe I've ever met—and the biggest hypocrite. You criticise my parents and yet they've always been there for me, even if they haven't always been there for each other. You have no right to pass judgement. You don't even know what commitment is. You just like control.'

'If you're not happy with how things are between us then all you have to do is say so,' he said, still with that frown carving deep into his forehead, his dark blue eyes as hard as black ice. 'I told you what I could offer. I didn't lie to you.

I made no promises. You came into this with your eyes wide open.'

Kitty should have backed away from the topic, but some inner demon demanded she push him regardless of the fall-out. She was tired of pretending she was OK with their arrangement. She wanted more. She wanted him to love her the way she had come to love him.

How could she *not* love him? She hadn't stood a chance right from the start. He had rocked her world the first time he had looked at her and smiled that dazzlingly sexy smile. What she had felt for Charles was nothing compared to what she felt for Jake. She was ashamed she had thought herself in love with her ex. It horrified her to think she would have married him and settled for such an insipid relationship. If what Sophie felt for Charles was even half of what she felt for Jake it was no wonder she had fallen into his arms the way she had. But, as much as she loved him, she didn't want to short-change herself in putting up with a relationship that was so out of balance. She would be a fool to think that in a few weeks there would be a tender, heartwarming airport scene where he would beg her to stay with him and marry him and have his babies.

No, he would probably wave her goodbye and then on his way home call up one of his 'friends with benefits'.

'I'm not as happy as I could be,' she said. 'And neither are you.'

He gave a harsh laugh. 'You think you know me so well, do you? Well, let me tell you I'm fine with my life right the way it is.'

'I think you want more out of life, but you're frightened of needing someone the way others need you,' she said. 'You've ruled out love because you don't want to be left like your mother was left, like *you* were left. You never got a chance to say goodbye to your father, did you? He just upped and left. You won't let that happen again. No one is going to tear your heart out again. No one. That's why it's always you who ends your relationships. You always get in first.'

A muscle moved like a hammer beneath the skin at the corner of his mouth. 'So,' he said, nailing her with his gaze, 'are you going to relieve me of the responsibility of calling it quits? Feel free. You'd be doing me a favour. This relationship has just about run its course.'

Kitty held his glittering gaze as pain at his cruel rejection moved through her body like a devastating poison. Her very bones ached with its toxicity. She had thought finding Sophie in Charles's arms had been crucifying, but it was nothing compared to this. How could he stand there and talk of their time together as if it meant absolutely nothing to him? Was she no more important than any other of his shallow hook-ups? She had foolishly thought she would win his heart. The last couple of weeks had given her hope that he was developing feelings for her. But she could see now his heart was never going to be available.

'It's over, Jake,' she said. 'I'm sorry but I can't be with you on your terms. I need more.'

'Still hankering after the boyfriend at home?' he said with a curl of his lip. 'I notice you're still wearing the ring. He's not going to come back to you. The sooner you accept that the better.'

She curled her fingers into her palm. 'I don't

want him to come back to me,' she said. 'I wouldn't take him back. I know now what I want. I know what I need. I'm not going to settle for second best.'

He held her gaze for a tense moment. A battle seemed to be going on behind his stone-like mask. She could see the micro-expressions on his face: a flicker of a pulse, the twitch of a muscle, the hardening of his eyes, and the hairpin-thinness of his lips.

'I guess that's it, then,' he said. 'I'll let you get on with your evening. I'll see you at work.'

Kitty's shoulders went down when the door clicked shut behind him. The sound seemed so much more than a lock slipping into place.

It was heartbreakingly, gut-wrenchingly *final*.

# CHAPTER SEVENTEEN

KITTY wasn't sure how she did it, but she got through the next couple of weeks with a courage she'd had no idea she possessed. She went to work and faced the speculation of the staff about her relationship with Jake with a poise she wouldn't have believed possible even a few weeks ago.

If Jake was upset by the termination of their brief affair he showed little sign of it. He was nothing but professional at work, although perhaps a little brusque on occasion, but Kitty kept her cool and continued to get through each day without letting him see how torn up she was. She had a particularly bad moment when she heard a rumour that he was interested in one of the nurses on the urology ward. But she never saw him bring anyone back to his place. He seemed to be working longer than normal hours, but then management had been putting a lot of pressure on keeping waiting times in A&E down.

As the date of Charles and Sophie's wedding approached, the ache Kitty had been so used to feeling about them gradually faded to a tiny pang for her fractured friendship rather than the stinging betrayal she had felt previously.

There was a bitter irony that it was Jake who had made her see the error of her ways. He had helped her to see how running away and feeling sorry for herself was not going to do anything but make her even more miserable, and how Charles's and Sophie's happiness would not be ruined by her dog-in-the-manger attitude.

He had called *her* selfish and immature, and yet what was *he* being?

She bit her lip to stop the tears from falling, as they were wont to do when she let her thoughts drift to him in unguarded moments.

She missed *everything* about him: his touch, his smell, his lazy smile and smouldering looks. She missed the closeness she had felt with him over the last few weeks.

Was she destined to be unhappy in love? Was

there something horribly wrong with her that no man would love her the way she needed to be loved?

The trouble was she didn't want any other man but Jake. How could she ever be with anyone else after all she had experienced with him? Her body *ached* for him. If she so much as caught a glimpse of him at work her flesh would contract and pulse with such intense longing it took her breath away.

Kitty looked at the pretty wedding invitation that had come in the post weeks ago. She picked it up and tapped it against her lips as she looked at the calendar on the fridge. She was rostered off for five days, which would give her just enough time to fly home and attend the service without compromising her commitment to the hospital.

She would support Charles and Sophie in their love for each other. She would be happy for them. She would celebrate with them—for she knew how precious it was to find a love that surpassed all others.

\* \* \*

As Kitty was packing her bag the evening before her flight she looked down at her promise ring. She must have lost weight in the last few days, for she could now turn it around on her finger. She went to the bathroom and soaped up her finger. It took an almighty effort, and her knuckle was probably going to be bruised and swollen as a result, but she finally got the ring off. She went back to the bedroom and slipped it inside the velvet lining of her jewellery case and gently closed the lid.

'What do you mean she's gone back to London?' Jake said to Gwen when he arrived at work on Wednesday morning. 'Why didn't she tell me she was leaving before her time was up?'

'Cool down, Jake,' Gwen said. 'She's coming back. She's only gone for a friend's wedding. She's rostered off for almost a week.'

Jake clenched his jaw. 'She should've told me she was leaving the country.'

'Why should she, Jake?' Gwen said. 'She's just another staff member. None of us have to tell you what we do in our private life. She could fly to Timbuktu on her days off and you couldn't do a thing about it.'

'I bet she doesn't come back,' he said, scowling at her furiously. 'She'll get over there and want to stay. You see if I'm not right.'

'And that would be a problem why, exactly?' Gwen asked with a raised-brow look.

Jake glowered at her. 'I'll be in my office if anyone wants me,' he said, and strode off down the corridor.

He sat brooding for an hour over paperwork. His concentration was shot. He couldn't believe Kitty had left the country without telling him. He'd only seen her the night before. Not that she had seen him. He had felt a bit like a MI5 spy or a sicko stalker, hiding behind the curtain in his kitchen, but how else was he to indulge his need to see her without her noticing his hang-dog look?

It was pathetic, that was what it was. He was turning out like some sort of lovesick fool.

*He was over her.*

It was time to move on. Start dating again. Have some fun.

He reached for his phone and scrolled through his contacts. There were at least seven women he could call for a drink. Tasha from Urology had cornered him in the cafeteria a week or so ago and he still hadn't got back to her. Maybe it was time to get back out there. He looked at Tasha's number. His finger hovered over the call button for a moment, but instead of pressing it he pressed delete.

He put his phone down on the desk but it rang almost immediately. He snatched it up and barked, 'Yes?'

'Whoa, no need to bite my head off,' said Rosie. 'Have I caught you at a bad time?'

He leaned back in his chair with a sigh. 'No,' he said. 'I'm just trawling through some paperwork that was meant to be done yesterday.'

'You don't sound happy,' Rosie said. 'Are you OK?'

'I'm fine.'

'You don't sound fine. You sound grumpy.'

'Yeah, well, I have a lot on my mind right now.'

'This is about Kitty, isn't it?' Rosie asked. 'Why did you guys call it quits? I thought she was perfect for you. To tell you the truth, Jake, she's the first girl you've dated that Jen and I have really liked. She'd make a fabulous sister-in-law. She's not a bimbo, for one thing. And don't forget she saved Robbie's life.'

'She's the one who broke it off,' he said, almost snapping the pen he'd picked up.

'So get back with her,' Rosie said. 'Tell her you want a second chance. Tell her you love her.'

He tossed the pen to one side. 'I'm not in love with her.'

Rosie laughed. 'Yeah, and I haven't got stretch marks. Come on, Jake. When have you been this smitten?'

'Smitten?' He recoiled at the term. 'I am *not* smitten.'

'You coughed up a thousand bucks for her,' Rosie said. 'You're smitten all right.'

Jake felt like throwing his phone at the wall. 'Did you have a reason for calling other than to rub my nose in the fact that I've been dumped?'

'I was hoping you could take Nathan for a couple of days,' Rosie said. 'You mentioned the other day at Robbie's that you've got this weekend off. It'll take your mind off things. I've got the chance to go to a health spa with a girlfriend. Should be fun.'

Jake drew in a breath and slowly exhaled. 'I was kind of hoping to have some time to myself this weekend.'

'You've been spending too much time by yourself lately,' Rosie said. 'Come on, Jake, it'll do you good to spend some quality time with Nathan. You've got nothing better to do, have you?'

Jake drummed his fingers on the desk for a moment. He could think of at least a hundred things he could do that would get him off the hook with his sister, but not one of them seemed important enough to justify spoiling her plans in order to indulge herself with a bit of R&R. The trouble was he was *always* putting other people's needs and wants before his own.

*And Kitty's.*

*Yeah, that's right, you great big bozo*, he

thought in self-recrimination. *Isn't it time you thought of what she wants and needs?*

Kitty was being brave enough to travel all that way to support her friends, to put her bitterness aside. Who would support her? Who would hand her tissue after tissue during the soppy bits of the service?

*Who would tell her he loved her and couldn't bear to spend another day without her in his life?*

Jake shoved back his chair and stood up. 'Actually, I do have something on,' he said. 'I'm flying to London for the weekend.'

'You're *what*?' Rosie gasped. 'Did you say London? London as in England? London as in Buckingham Palace and Big Ben and the Queen and Harrods?'

'Yep.'

'Are you out of your cotton-picking mind? Rosie asked. 'Who on earth flies to London for a *weekend*?'

Jake felt a smile spread over his face. 'A man head over heels in love does,' he said, and hung up the phone.

* * *

'You look beautiful,' Kitty said as she adjusted Sophie's veil outside the church. 'I'm so happy for you.'

Sophie gripped Kitty's hands in both of hers. 'I'm so glad you came,' she said with tears in her eyes. 'It means so much to Charles and me. We could never be happy together unless we felt you were happy for us.'

'I *am* happy for you,' Kitty said. 'I'm sorry for being such a cow about things. I can't believe I was so childish. You two belong together. Anyone can see that.'

Sophie beamed. 'Here's our cue,' she said as the organ started to play. 'Shall we get this show on the road?'

'Let's do it.' Kitty smiled even though a part of her ached that Jake wasn't here to see how brave she was being. She missed him more now there were so many miles between them.

*But then he had always been far away—if not physically then emotionally.*

Jake's flight was late landing, and then there was a delay coming through Customs. He had to wait ages for a taxi, and to top it all off there was an accident a kilometre or so from the church where the wedding was taking place. He had sourced that information via Gwen, who had let slip that Kitty's best friend was being married in her home village just outside of London.

The service was well under way by the time he trudged through the snow, having paid off the taxi driver who had had no choice but to stick it out until the tow trucks cleared everything away.

It was *freezing*.

How did anyone survive this climate? His face felt as if it was being burned with the cold. The sun was like a rheumy eye behind moody clouds. Why would anyone get married on a day like this? Why not wait until spring or summer, when there was at least the faint possibility of the sun breaking through the mattress-thick clouds?

Jake slipped in the back of the church and watched the proceedings. Kitty was standing holding the bride's bouquet. She looked amazing. She was wearing a blue V-neck satin dream of a tea dress that clung to her slim body like a glove. Her hair was in an up style that highlighted her elegant cheekbones. Her make-up was understated, but she still outshone the bride.

Quite frankly, he couldn't see what the groom was thinking in choosing the bride over Kitty. The bride looked OK—well, more than OK if you had a thing for straight raven hair and strong features. Kitty, on the other hand looked delicate and dainty. She had a smile on her face that he could only hope was genuine.

A flood of doubts suddenly assailed him. What if she sent him packing? What if he made a complete fool of himself before all these toffee-nosed guests?

He started to picture it in his head. A top-notch security team would frogmarch him to the door, shoving him out into the cold...

But then Kitty shifted slightly and locked gazes with him. He saw the shock in her eyes. They opened wide, along with her mouth, but then, as if she suddenly remembered she had a role to play as maid of honour, she turned back to the proceedings and fixed a neutral smile on her face.

Jake glanced at the ushers either side of him at

the back of the church. So far so good. He wasn't identified as an interloper—yet.

The bride and groom kissed and then moved to the vestry to sign the register. Kitty went with the rest of the bridal party. Jake's insides clenched when he saw the best man slide his arm around her waist in a proprietorial manner.

He wanted to punch the guy's lights out.

The bride and groom were announced and began to make their journey back down the aisle. Jake waited patiently as Kitty went past. She sent him a sideways glance that made his heart race. Was that a smile he could see playing about her lips? Was it for the cameras or for him?

He had to wait twenty minutes or so to find out. Finally he cornered her in between photos. 'Hi,' he said. 'Nice day for a wedding.'

'You think?' Kitty said with a wary look.

'Personally I'd opt for a summer day at the beach, with a celebrant in bare feet,' he said. 'Just a few close friends and family. And a barbecue in the park to follow—a few beers, loads of cheap champagne.'

She angled her head at him. 'No cucumber sandwiches?'

He grinned at her. 'Maybe a couple, if that's what you want.'

Her neat brows met over her eyes. 'Are you...?' She shook her head as if she was hallucinating. 'God, I knew I shouldn't have had that champagne with Sophie while we were getting our hair done. It's gone straight to my head.'

'I love you,' Jake said. 'I want to marry you.'

Kitty blinked. 'I am never going to let alcohol pass my lips again. *Ever.*' She made to move past him. 'Excuse me. I have to join the others for the official photos. They're waiting for me.'

'Hey,' Jake said, snaring her arm to bring her back to face him. 'I've just travelled close to seventeen thousand kilometres to ask you to marry me. The least you could do is give me a straight yes or no.'

Kitty ran her tongue over her lips. 'Is this a joke?' she asked. 'Are you doing this to make fun of me or something?'

He barked out a wry laugh. 'You think I'd joke about something like this? I left everything to

284 DR CHANDLER'S SLEEPING BEAUTY

get over here to be with you. I'll probably lose my job when the CEO finds out I've left the country. I just wanted to see you face-to-face. I've never asked someone to marry me before. I didn't want to do it over the phone or with a text or on Skype. Telling someone you love them is a big deal—or at least it is in my book.'

Kitty felt a tremor of sheer joy judder through her body. 'You love me?'

His sapphire-blue gaze softened. 'How could I *not* love you?' he asked, grasping her by the hands. 'I want to spend the rest of my life with you. Marry me, Kitty. Have babies with me. I'll be a great dad. I've had loads of practice. I'm not sure what sort of husband I'll make. I haven't had a great role model. But I know I love you so much that I can't bear the thought of spending another day of my life without you in it.'

Kitty was reeling from shock, surprise and happiness. 'But I thought you never wanted to get married,' she said. 'You said you didn't want to be tied down. That you were sick of being re-sponsible for everyone.'

'Loving someone is all about responsibility,'

Jake said. 'As soon as you love someone you become responsible for them and they become responsible for you. I've been watching out for my family for so long that I didn't realise I was part of the problem. My sisters and brother are so used to me being there for them that they've forgotten how to be there for each other. With me stepping away for these few days Rosie has turned to Jen for help. Robbie has chipped in as well.'

Kitty looked at him in wonder, still not sure if she was imagining him standing before her in person. 'I can't believe you came all this way,' she said. 'I keep thinking you're going to melt away in a puff of smoke or something.'

'*Smoke?*' He looked at her incredulously. 'Are you joking? I'm more likely to be frozen to the spot. How on earth do you live like this? It's perishingly cold out here, and there you are with bare arms and shoulders. Do you want my jacket?' He quickly shrugged himself out of it and draped it around her shoulders.

She smiled as she breathed in his scent and body warmth. 'I just want you,' she said.

He cupped her face in his hands and pressed a lingering kiss to her mouth. 'God, I've missed you *so* much,' he said, once he had raised his mouth off hers. 'You *are* coming back, aren't you? You still have six weeks to fulfil your term.'

Her eyes danced as they held his. 'So I'm not on probation any more, Dr Chandler?' she asked.

He tugged her up close, his eyes glinting down at her. 'You never were,' he said and captured her mouth beneath his.

\* \* \* \* \*

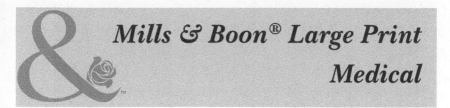

# *Mills & Boon® Large Print*
# *Medical*

## June

| | |
|---|---|
| FROM CHRISTMAS TO ETERNITY | Caroline Anderson |
| HER LITTLE SPANISH SECRET | Laura Iding |
| CHRISTMAS WITH DR DELICIOUS | Sue MacKay |
| ONE NIGHT THAT CHANGED EVERYTHING | Tina Beckett |
| CHRISTMAS WHERE SHE BELONGS | Meredith Webber |
| HIS BRIDE IN PARADISE | Joanna Neil |

## July

| | |
|---|---|
| THE SURGEON'S DOORSTEP BABY | Marion Lennox |
| DARE SHE DREAM OF FOREVER? | Lucy Clark |
| CRAVING HER SOLDIER'S TOUCH | Wendy S. Marcus |
| SECRETS OF A SHY SOCIALITE | Wendy S. Marcus |
| BREAKING THE PLAYBOY'S RULES | Emily Forbes |
| HOT-SHOT DOC COMES TO TOWN | Susan Carlisle |

## August

| | |
|---|---|
| THE BROODING DOC'S REDEMPTION | Kate Hardy |
| AN INESCAPABLE TEMPTATION | Scarlet Wilson |
| REVEALING THE REAL DR ROBINSON | Dianne Drake |
| THE REBEL AND MISS JONES | Annie Claydon |
| THE SON THAT CHANGED HIS LIFE | Jennifer Taylor |
| SWALLOWBROOK'S WEDDING OF THE YEAR | Abigail Gordon |

# Mills & Boon® Large Print
## Medical

## September

| | |
|---|---|
| NYC ANGELS: REDEEMING THE PLAYBOY | Carol Marinelli |
| NYC ANGELS: HEIRESS'S BABY SCANDAL | Janice Lynn |
| ST PIRAN'S: THE WEDDING! | Alison Roberts |
| SYDNEY HARBOUR HOSPITAL: EVIE'S BOMBSHELL | Amy Andrews |
| THE PRINCE WHO CHARMED HER | Fiona McArthur |
| HIS HIDDEN AMERICAN BEAUTY | Connie Cox |

## October

| | |
|---|---|
| NYC ANGELS: UNMASKING DR SERIOUS | Laura Iding |
| NYC ANGELS: THE WALLFLOWER'S SECRET | Susan Carlisle |
| CINDERELLA OF HARLEY STREET | Anne Fraser |
| YOU, ME AND A FAMILY | Sue MacKay |
| THEIR MOST FORBIDDEN FLING | Melanie Milburne |
| THE LAST DOCTOR SHE SHOULD EVER DATE | Louisa George |

## November

| | |
|---|---|
| NYC ANGELS: FLIRTING WITH DANGER | Tina Beckett |
| NYC ANGELS: TEMPTING NURSE SCARLET | Wendy S. Marcus |
| ONE LIFE CHANGING MOMENT | Lucy Clark |
| P.S. YOU'RE A DADDY! | Dianne Drake |
| RETURN OF THE REBEL DOCTOR | Joanna Neil |
| ONE BABY STEP AT A TIME | Meredith Webber |